There Is No Was

Vicente James Hernandez

Onion Scribe Publishing

Cover & Interior Design by Scribe Freelance | www.scribefreelance.com

Cover photograph and manipulation by Bill Havranek

ISBN: 978-0-9835435-3-4

www.thereisnowas.com

Published in the United States of America

. . . time is a fluid condition which has no existence except in the momentary avatars of individual people. There is no such thing as *was*—only *is*. If *was* existed, there would be no grief or sorrow.

—WILLIAM FAULKNER

PROLOGUE
The Boy Becomes the Man

It is happening—the question he asks his mother as a child is being answered by his life: How do you grow up?

And when does this happen?

The answer she gives is perfect: When you aren't thinking about it.

And so that is how it occurs—without his noticing, his attention diverted by his own life, a betrayal inside him, but a necessary one, one bound to happen, a betrayal from which everything else after can be allowed.

The boy becomes the man, something in his head cracking open, somewhere along the timeline of all things before the moment and, of course, after it.

Though, later on, he is unable to relocate the event in his memory in any conventional sense or through any method available to his brain awake, though he is not precisely able to *remember* what has happened, he senses that some secret part of him knows.

Some part of him possesses the knowledge of his changing. It is the instrument that strings his existence along, so of course it knows, of course it remembers, of course the thing buried underneath the rest of him recalls the moment.

The moment that the crackle ripples through his thick, squirming brain and travels into his blood and, through there, travels into all of him, turning itself inside out, folding him and folding him.

And unfolding him and, instantaneously and at the cost of his original form, he is new.

Because how else?

How else anything?

His original form—

Thirteen years removed from the day he is born, he is in a waterpark. Chlorine unnatural as poison floods the air. Ironically, the first waterpark he has visited since preadolescence is in the middle of the desert. Treading water angelically in front of him—a girl who is more beautiful than his mind can grasp. Every time he thinks he grasps her beauty he loses hold again to the shape of her body, the movement of her. Her beauty is a woman's even though her body is only a year older than Walter's.

Walter and Katherine are in a wave pool in a waterpark in the middle of the desert, both joined and separated by their sex, their stupid, stupid age—hovering over each other but not touching, glued to the air by the sticky heat, the oily smell of overly applied sunscreen, the sweat of random people. The crowd of middle-aged men, women, married and adult in the depressing settledness of them and their freckled, hairy chests; the elderly in their sagging skin exposed, reptilian and ripe for shedding; children of all ages darting through the maze of blue plaster with the attention of squirrels; and even Walter and Katherine's peers—young, fearing God, loud and happy and outgoing and *together*. A *group*. They are separated by the very people they came here with, carried from the suburbs of North Carolina in a commercial airliner to the uncompromising desert of Arizona.

To save souls.

Theirs or others.

But mostly theirs.

Walking through the crusted dust of dilapidated neighborhoods, where they are alone. Rebuilding the foundations to a house. Doing *good*.

They wash off the dust in the bitter afternoon heat, but the morning crust in their eyes is part of them. The eye crust tucked too deep for even the blue water to reach into them and pry out with freshness.

They are dirty.

They are dirty and the dirt comes off them in soft grey clouds drifting through the artificial bright blue of the pool water.

The waves haven't started yet. They smile at each other. Walter darts underwater, again overwhelmed at Katherine's astonishing prettiness. The feeling rolls inside, pushing him under, in control. How strange to have this thing from within controlling him, but utterly not him—Katherine, incipient woman, infection of the air that slipped in through his eyes and dug into him, not stopping until reaching his core.

Kat is what she goes by, but he thinks of her as Katherine: Kat is too short a name for her, too much of a chirp. The little nickname doesn't roll through him when he thinks about her, moving along the lips too easily. Nothing about her is easy. For him she is a trap.

The youth leader, an oldish boy, calling out their full names proper and each one a bullet fired, precise and full, with a body.

Katherine.

He will not forget her.

CHAPTER I
The Eyes Were Grey

Underwater, Walter's eyes were squeezed shut, childishly stubborn in their insistence not to open. He defied them and ripped his eyes open and felt the glorious pain of chlorine pour through his sockets. He saw everything for the first time.

He saw her—

His vision enhanced through submersion, her silhouette glowing, shadow and light swirling about her, her beauty elevated to myth—she was a mermaid plucked from ancient times.

He observed her thighs sprouting from the bottom of her bikini in flourishing, round shapes. His beating eyes followed the transition of her thighs all the way from her knees to her calves to her ankles to the wrinkled bottoms of her feet and finally to her wiggling, mismatched toes. Her legs hovered above him, heavenly, fanning him, moving back and forth. It was hypnotic. He studied them and the intricacies of their design until he was certain that her body was the greatest thing he had witnessed. He waited below for an eternity.

Finally the pleasure of the moment transformed to torture and he reached out.

Her skin was soft to touch, even behind the sluggish disguise of the water.

He rose to the surface ashamed, almost ready to ignore her, anything to expel his failure in the face of temptation. He wondered if maybe she would pretend the lustful clutching of her thigh had been brought on by the movement of the artificial waves.

But no—the waves hadn't started yet. The pool now sat still.

He couldn't resist making eye contact with her.

She narrowed her eyes and turned a devilish smile on him.

She touched his bony shoulder with a wet hand.

Her eyes were grey, as if shaded in with pencil, unafraid and comfortably still in their sockets.

"Walt," she said, adapting the husky voice of a woman twice her age, "you *are* cute," putting the tone in all the right places to make him remember, to stamp the moment in his mind.

His shoulder smarted, warmly, beneath the skin.

Kat. Katherine.

At least a year later, Walter would spend an entire night awake because he remembered her.

His mother had pushed him into going on the mission trip to Arizona with the church youth group, insisting he had no friends, no connection, no key for the door behind which his peers waited.

At first he regretted caving into the decision, struggling with the sledgehammer they gave him, heaving the massive thing through the air and into the rusted beginnings from which—he could not believe—a home would be forged. The ground stared up at him, crafted of the dust that had invaded the air, igniting his allergies, irritating him, weaving through his nasal passage and struggling to become a part of him.

Walter and the older counselor figure, Andrew, took a water break under the shade of a tree nearby.

Not old enough to be entirely adult, but old enough to sit beside Walter without reservation, relaxing, not needing to pretend, Andrew said nothing and his silence made Walter twitch into speech.

"I don't understand."

"What don't you understand, Walt?" Andrew emptied the last of his water bottle over himself and his white tank turned grey where the water invaded the cottony hill of his chest.

"I thought *they* would be here," Walter said, approaching the line between a voice and a child's whine.

The young man shook his head and a sprinkle of water showered down, several sharp drops sticking to Walter's cheek. Not cool, the water sizzled at his face like acid threatening to singe his skin.

"Who would be here?"

One drenched dollop of his bleach blonde hair stuck out, sculpted, an arrow pointing to Walter.

Walter frowned. He wiped his cheek. "I don't know."

Words tumbled from him. The possibility that he was about to open up to Andrew was dangerously near. Walter wanted to be a wall to everyone, the boy behind it not even visible. But—despite his shyness—he wasn't.

He was at war with his insides and always needed a new recruit.

He continued: "I thought *they* would be here. The people we were helping. I wanted them to thank me. For what we're doing for them."

The young man rolled back his head by the neck and laughed, restraining no piece of his reaction for Walter's naïve sake. He was usually gentle. When his laughter had subsided, Andrew prepared himself to use that gentleness, taking a deep breath. "Do you remember what Pastor James says?" he posed eagerly. "About when we get to heaven?"

Walter tried to force the image of Pastor James into his mind, but nothing came. He could faintly sense that this man existed and he had seen him before and he thought maybe he was bald, but other than that—nothing. "No," he said, ashamed slightly. His mother and he barely attended church on Christmas and Easter.

"When we get to heaven," Andrew explained slowly with deliberateness, a conviction afforded to those who were certain of their logic, "everyone we ever helped will be there. Every single one. There will be people we didn't even *know* we helped. They will all be there to thank us. Unless, of course, they went to the other place, that is."

"Oh," Walter said, defeated, just as the image of the pastor seemed to be faintly attainable in his mind, his bald head shining. "I see."

They waited for nothing to happen, for the moment to pass,

the sun reaching under the shadow of the tree to beat them senseless, to suck the water from their pores, to steal their body-fuel.

Walter did not want to stand up. But he did. He grabbed his sledgehammer.

"But hell isn't real," he said, to himself, almost not aloud. He seemed to have pulled himself up from sitting position with these words.

"Oh hell is real," said Andrew, calmly, lazy-eyed, assuming his place alongside Walter and readying himself to construct.

"No," Walter said. "It's not." He dropped the sledgehammer at Andrew's certainness and stared ahead, struggling to peel his eyes open wider. The sun invaded his vision, turned his sight to a golden, dusty fog. The desert had assimilated them without as much as noticing their presence.

"It's real," Andrew said, continuing to work.

"My mom said it isn't real." Walter actually didn't think she had, but he was certain this was a good argument, solid reasoning.

Andrew stopped working again so he could corner the boy, looking at him long enough to drive home this point. "It *is* real. It is a place where there isn't anything other than suffering. People go there all the time. People are sometimes bad, Walter, and God punishes them. That's how things are, that's how things are supposed to be. It's in the Bible, and the Bible is real. It describes things that are real and that really happened. And that are *going* to happen."

Walter's mind had drifted into his oncoming fear. He saw hell, the image growing as his reasoning faded in the face of Andrew's certainty. He heard the screams of tortured souls. Then maybe they couldn't breathe or scream, maybe their mouths were sewn shut.

"How can you be so sure?"

Andrew shrugged. "There are people who have been there. People whose hearts stopped and then they were revived. They've described it. You can read about it. There was a man who wrote a book. I think he said it was like a white empty room with nothing in it. He died when he was thirty, but in the room he is very, very old. Maybe a hundred. He is so skinny and old his skin is kind of hanging from him. There is a bowl of soup in front of him and he is starving, but he can't bend over to get to it. He is just staring at it."

Walter gulped. He thought of his moment of temptation before and Katherine and all the things he wanted to do to her and all the things he had imagined doing to her the night before, sleeping on the floor of the church, huddled in a tangle of blankets, holding himself and thinking and believing he was safe in his aloneness.

Andrew went back to work, moving his hammer as naturally as an extension of his body, a swinging, overheavy third arm.

Walter—youngest and most innocent of the group. The first kiss of his short life came when Kat leaned the wet softness of her lips into his right cheek as they said goodbye, back at the church in North Carolina, each one of them waiting for parents to arrive and steal them from their adventure. The gesture had started out as a friendly hug but had become something uncharted, dangerous, new. Walter's face like hot sand. He opened his mouth and then shut it, afraid to speak in this new world he had entered.

What a trip, he said softly to himself that night, reaccepted by the loving, slightly cool linen of his bed, waiting to hear the comfortable sound of his mother's insomnia, her feet patting the floor in an order of thumps he had memorized as she drifted through the house in search of a window to shove her face into and stare out.

He heard the door to her bedroom creak and sighed with a deep relief.

School was another thing entirely. While it approached, stomping away in the distance—ominous and threatening—the summer closed behind him, an organic opening that collapsed with a gurgle.

School came, and he was inside a shadowy cave.

His days had been unnamed, open-ended—boring but full of potential. After returning from the desert, summer days consisted of Cap'n Crunch for breakfast, lunch and dinner; falling asleep with a Super Nintendo controller in hand before the afternoon was through; wandering the neighborhood by himself, head hung, beady eyes swinging to the approaching bikini-clad neighborhood teenage girl on her way to the nearest watering hole—the swimming pool down the street. Her flip flops slapped the street, a melodic threat to his head.

Now, his school days consisted of willing the hands on the antique styled clock in the upper corner of the classroom to tick more rapidly in its achingly consistent movement, to signal the end of the day, bring him freedom.

He watched his teachers with sparkling, attentive eyes. He was stupidly hopeful. When other students asked if they could copy his homework, he politely declined. He was called *teacher's pet* without an eye batting.

The worst was that he saw Katherine. From far away. A nagging memory of a life lived previously. She was a grade ahead and in none of his classes, thankfully, for then she would discover the fear that kept him closed off to his peers, she would witness his nakedness, his social awkwardness, his inability to do anything in a way that allowed him to disappear mercifully into a crowd of those his age.

He went to the cafeteria as the clock hands signaled the appropriate time and as the teacher unleashed them on each other, students cruelly sniffling at each other and calling out dangerous slurs—words much older than they, created or altered with the adult intent to hate. They inherited the hate by no decision of their own, already in their blood, hiding there, peeking out at moments when the word *faggot, trailer trash* or *nigger* was whispered or screamed, each mutilation of language waiting for an excuse to make its presence felt.

The school was dirty, down to every corner, with shed hairs and cockroach carcasses and the chemical smell of some dried fluid, probably urine, and a hoarding nest of some creature, an overgrown rat perhaps, mutated. The cafeteria was no exception. Discarded, uneaten food everywhere, condiment packets leaking their half-congealed slime across the tables. Students chewed with their open, laughing mouths spilling bits of food. Gluttony and poverty reigned together, somehow in harmony.

Walter ate at a table by himself, positioned out of sight, but with Katherine in view. He watched her voluptuous lips move up and down as food was put in between them. A boy, older than he, the beginnings of a beard sprouting from his cheeks and neck, sat beside her, close, leaning in to tell her something.

What was he whispering to her, what secret did he impart to her?

Who was he and what was his name?

Was he—Walter almost choked on his soggy fries—her *boyfriend?*

He watched the pair. The look on his face was controlled as a hired hit man, detached from them as if some silhouette of a criminal had handed him a wad of bills to sit there and watch. He was simply following instructions.

Right before the bell rang and lunch was dismissed, the two of them parted. She kissed him on a bearded cheek.

Walter put a hand to his forehead, not aware of the motion, feeling the hurt beat quietly beneath the skin.

By way of graciousness, for relief from the tension, or just to move into a new kind of grueling torture, Walter was again noticed by her.

Recess—he sat in the discomfort of a rusty bench. The heavy, violent rhythm of the gigantic basketball players swayed before him on the outdoor court. They were Greek gods battling over mankind—no, just squabbling, in disagreement of their anger and power. The squeak of their sneakers on the court shrieked at him, bolts of lightning. He twitched.

She slipped next to him on the bench, soft and quiet. Looking over, he was startled. She said his name and smiled modestly, flashing the white of her teeth. He wanted to pull apart her lips and almost had to sit on his hands.

"Walter."

He spoke without breathing, a wheeze, a gulp—what combination of water and vocal cords and noise inside him made a voice?

"Katherine," he sputtered.

"I haven't seen you in forever. I didn't know you went to school here."

"Oh," he said.

"Where have you been? What do you do on Sundays?"

"Oh." He looked to his tennis shoes for aid, felt the presence of his feet underneath the dirty, spoiled rubbery white of them. "I don't know. My mom doesn't really go to church much."

"But you went with us to Arizona. On the mission trip." She looked at him sadly, and he saw the innocent lack of malice in her eyes and felt the suffering she put inside of him.

"My mom thought it would be good for me."

"You should come on Sundays. The youth group meets on Sunday nights."

She reached out to his shoulder and picked a piece of grass from his sweatshirt and flicked the yellowed shred to the ground. October now. He stopped breathing for long enough to count to three, then he started breathing again. He watched his breath flow from him, solid, the discovery of this invisible thing revealed in the cold—camouflage spoiled.

"I don't think I will be able to come to that."

She turned her smile to a frown, just for him. "Why not?"

He was touched by the sweetness of her, the caring. "I just don't think my mom would bother to take me." He forced a sigh down with great effort.

He watched her face for a moment, unable not to. "You have something on your chin."

She wiped her face.

"No. It's still there. Wait. What is that? It's red, it's all over."

He saw himself holding her face and kissing the rash away, in a bright green field, white horses galloping near them. Each time he pulled his mouth away from her face the skin was new there.

"Oh." Her cheeks turned to blood. "It's—it's from my boyfriend. His beard rubs me when we, uh." There was a pause within which Walter might have ceased existing.

"I have to go." She stood up.

He ran a finger along the rusty corner of the bench and felt it flake against his skin.

That night, very awake in his bed, he cupped his naked chin in his palm, rubbing it and thought how stupid and babyish his skin was, so smooth, so clean, so blank.

■ ■ ■

She noticed him this time at lunch, the vacant cafeteria table he sat at stretching out before him as long as a football field after the game let out, unpeopled and green and huge and barren. She sat next to him for a moment.

"Why do you eat by yourself, Walt?"

"What?"

"You're all alone."

"Oh. My friend just went to the bathroom, he'll be back in a second."

"Who is that?"

"Who?"

"Your friend. Who is it?"

"Huh?"

She shook her head in swift confusion. "Why don't you both come sit with us?"

"Okay. I guess so."

Walter followed her with the disposition of a beaten dog to the table where her bearded boyfriend sat, fries spilling halfway out his mouth.

The echo of suffocating awkwardness followed Walter, no words were exchanged, silence reigned.

Right after leading him to the table, Katherine turned to leave Walter alone with her boyfriend, and she was getting dessert or using the restroom or—as Walter suspected—simply creating a horrifically uncomfortable moment at his expense. He decided there still was a chance that she, in fact, exploited his weakness for her, deliberately torturing him.

He could not hate her.

He stared at the older boy's chin.

The older boy gulped. "Hey."

Walter stared on.

"Hey. I'm Mike."

"Oh. I'm Walt."

"Are you sick or something?"

Walter shook his head. "No. No. I just—" He whittled away a risky second, daring himself to ask and then feeling himself doing it. "What's it feel like to have a beard?"

"A beard? I don't know. It itches." He scratched at his ragged, hairy mess of a cheek and crammed three more fries into his mouth.

▪ ▪ ▪

October down—the vicious plunge of a hunter duck, scouring for fish but not surfacing immediately as you expected.

November too came and went.

Christmas, with that overload of attention and the sparkling tint of his mother's eyes under her eggnog veil. Christmas and His well-known music and His bubbling over of warmth planted in all of them without their knowing—covert, secret, to distract them from any *real* meaning. Family he didn't really know slept in his bed and turned the smell of his sheets unpleasant, a distinct violation of familiarity.

His uncle. His Uncle Ralph. His stench was like peanut butter and thick when it oozed on you. No, no, no, he felt a rise in himself, a rebellion. Everything pointless.

His father did not come this year.

■ ▨ ▦

He returned to school in January a boy defeated, unable to look his teachers in the face. He lost track of his life with the same heartbreak you would lose your infant's hand on a crowded street. Where was his waterpark now? Those things happened in another lifetime. He was numb and yet even his numbness hurt somehow.

"Walter," Mrs. Malseed addressed his indifference in class, "Walter?"

He stirred from his melancholic daydream angrily, reorienting himself at his desk, squeezing the number two pencil in his palm, the thick lead like smelling salts to his drifting mind. "What?"

"Answer the question."

He paused. "What was the question?" he asked as casually as if he weren't supposed to know.

Malseed's face turned crooked, wrinkled in slight concern. She moved in on Walter's desk, the old woman stink of her breath on him when she finally spoke again. "Are you on drugs?"

"No," he answered, in this case truth also being the correct answer.

He had almost given up.

He continued for a while like this, in this stage.

At least a few days, a week?

Time had no meaning really.

He resolved himself at last to infiltrate the world of boys and girls around him. This was the year—1999 with the millennium rolling around the corner and the end of the world on the rise, again a beginning for everyone: the beginning of the end. If there was no hope for everyone else, could that mean there was hope for him? This could be it, the time he broke through the utter pitifulness of his life.

His time had come, to become a part of his culture, to be one of them. He would find peace in acceptance from his peers.

He had observed them carefully from the outside, like a man with his palm pressed to the glass of an enclosed miniature world, watching the beings inside grow and play amongst each other, unable to participate. But not anymore. He had been taking notes—

He forced himself to watch his first rap music video from beginning to end on the television. He was surprised—now paying attention—at the happiness, the spectacle. An explosion of colors that seemed in danger of sizzling the screen. Sparks from all corners. The iconic image, eternal, the shape of a woman's body, already burned into his brain, danced before him. The green spandex of their decadent masquerade quietly blew his mind. How had this not already been his religion? How had the culture of this music escaped him until this moment? Better late than never, he reflected.

The silvery green wear glistened on the dancers' bodies like grease on a fat-saturated meal of fast food and sort of felt connected to that, whipped up with factory-style haste at the demand of the public who waited hungrily, frothing at the mouth, devouring without pausing to note the flavor.

The subjects of the video pranced about the golden backdrop of Las Vegas, crotches always the focus of the screen, clownish clothes hanging from them, heads the most shrunken part, distantly bobbing at the top of the screen, strangely small due to the skewed perspective.

He found a tape cassette nestled in the crust of the sidewalk on the way to the school bus stop one morning. He looked at the dirty tape and then looked away, just long enough to consider it, as it slid into his pocket. He felt like he was doing something bad, like someone had seen him and was going to tell on him.

He touched the plastic texture of the thing in his pocket as the school day went by, five hours at a time, each hour tearing through him.

Back home, school at last snubbed out, he hunted through piles of clothes in his mother's room, gritting his teeth each time he discovered panties and discarding them between the delicate pinch of two fingers, and he came upon what he searched for finally—his mother's Walkman, the only time she had any use for it once upon a morning when she would put on running shorts and jog through the mildly humid mist of the unrisen sun.

The music that came through the headphones was exactly the right kind, rap music, forbidden debauchery, drumbeat driven head nodding, nodding he was yet to feel in his blood, but he had witnessed the bobbing necks of other boys on the bus, behind their headphones and their unheard rap.

Listening closely, he discovered that he loved this music, despite that—and also *because* it was a brutal representation of everything he could never convincingly be.

The lyrics taught him words he hadn't known existed, sharp and offensive even when he lacked the meaning in the machine gun action of their delivery spoken with nastiness, an appreciation for the sharp edge to them.

He mouthed them to himself, the door to the bathroom shut and locked, watching his lips move in the mirror.

He tossed a handful of them to a boy on the bus, his voice dropping to a whisper, moving over the monosyllabic shape of each one—

Those hoes at the front of the bus can suck my dick.

The boy ignored him, unblinking, maybe not hearing that words were spoken in his direction, an unlit cigarette hanging from his lips. He sat next to Walter but talked heavily with the group of boys sitting behind them.

Walter saw that his jeans sagged, clamped below his waist by his belt, a silver logo trailing down the side of the black denim, his colorful, plaid boxers visible, the look of him stepping out of a music video.

"I need new clothes, Mom," he reported at the silence of the kitchen table, looking up from his untouched plate of microwaved broccoli. The plate smelled green, like green had turned itself to a scent and the results were horrific. His mother was standing in the kitchen, plateless herself, humming as she went about.

"You have clothes," she answered, barely needing to break from the tune swimming in her mind.

"I need *new* clothes. All my clothes have holes in them."

She tucked the bottom half of her lip into her mouth, biting, staring him down, reflecting or either trying not to.

They were in the mall a week later, that huge emptiness always overwhelming to Walter, emptiness outweighing crowds of people violently shopping, and he struggled to grow up in the face of it, to insist he was old enough.

She yanked his hand into hers.

Walter ripped his fingers from his mother's clutch—disgusted, frowning deeper than his mouth would allow.

"You're still my boy," his mother said. A grin took over her face. Her dimples stretched her loose skin to the limits and he looked up at her and saw that her face consisted of innumerable wrinkles. She was older than the Bible.

The men's section. A valley away in JCPenney, several heartbeats and an escalator from where they stood. She was unbudging, but so was he.

"You are big, Honey. Just not *that* big."

The nerves under his skin sparked, catching fire. "I'm getting clothes from there. Or we are leaving *now*."

She looked down at him, he could not have patted her head without standing on a stool. From his youthful eyes she witnessed his anger, almost as afraid for herself as she was for him, in awe of the rawness.

"I'm waiting," he said.

She felt a sigh coming that she swallowed, not without

difficulty. She saw the tiny face, a younger version of him, playing dress up in his father's drooping clothes, the slack of them almost threatening to suffocate him.

"Okay," she said at last.

It's Saturday, she thought, he doesn't have school tomorrow—tonight I'll drink myself to sleep, she reflected with comfort. But—in the event that alcohol served to move her into a state of hyper-alertness—there were pills for that, hidden from sight, buried in the same dresser drawer as her underwear to safeguard against accidental discovery.

He came out of the dressing room in clothes clinging to his body as loose as a heavy animal curled up around him.

"It's too big," she said nastily.

■ ■ ■

On Monday, Walter strolled into school clothed as a man, stumbling and clumsy in his new wear, a criminal tripping into his own noose, meant just for him, prepared and arranged in anticipation of his next move. Snagged, he tripped and fell in front of his peers, in front of the lockers, in the hallway, creating the opposite effect intended—laughter coming at him in a devastating attack.

He waited for the others to notice him at lunch, he strutted through the line as the cafeteria ladies piled slop onto his tray, he displayed his jeans with a turn or a rotation that caused them to stand out just right, his new shirt, he was the rapper in the video, he was at the center of the world, demanding your attention.

"Aren't my new pants cool?" Walter ventured from the emptiness of his usual table, setting his tray hopefully beside a random peer.

The boy stared back at Walter with the look of the drugged. Mute and mesmerized by his own mind state.

"I'm Walter. I think you're in one of my classes."

The dumb look of the boy sunk in for a pulse-pounding

second. Long enough for two heartbeats to pass. "You're a faggot." He spoke matter of fact, mouth wide open, displaying a small, yellow pile of food on one side of his tongue. He scooted down the table, away from Walter, chewing his food along the way with seemingly practiced nonchalance.

His attempt at assimilation a failure.

Flat out.

On his way home from the bus stop, strolling down the road, kicking a little rock and then kicking it again once he caught up with it, and then kicking it again until the rock was gone forever. He went too close to the rickety fence of a neighbor when a nail protruded and caught his jeans. Ripping.

He put a hand to his thigh and felt skin where there should have been denim. He swallowed the possibility of tears and kept walking, speaking to himself gently, carefully, practiced by now, here I am.

What now?

What else was there?

Nothing.

* * *

He discovered a book, *Brave New World*, aging on his mother's coffee table, wiping the dust off with the inside of his palm. The spine was a mossy green color, a crease running down the center that marked where the last reader had left off—the book at least half spoiled, unvirgin. The cover had a black and white photo of the author. This man looked locked away in a time two hundred years ago, a time the world had long left, unpausing in its progress to look back at him. He skipped the foreword automatically, read the opening lines and was done for.

He carried the book to his room, not looking up the entire way there.

His mother came to get him in the morning, to prepare him for school. She smelled of rotted chemicals that were poisonous, something dangerous, something to avert your nose from, something the doctor used to knock out his patients with, wearing a mask to guard from the potency. Walter was a hundred pages in and had forgotten about having a mother, her presence now only annoying.

"Your light is on," she said suspiciously. "Why would your light be on?"

He looked up at her from his spot on the unmade bed. "Because I never went to sleep."

"My god."

"You didn't sleep either."

"That's not true."

"You didn't sleep. I can hear you, you know. Walking around the house like it's daytime, talking on the phone. Or maybe just talking to yourself."

"That's not true, that's ridiculous."

"Whatever," he said, lifting the book back over him, shoving his face deep into it.

⬛ ⬛ ⬛

He put his head on his desk at school and went to sleep. Dark fog turned sentient and crawled through him and converted his mind, conquering him. Mrs. Malseed observed him with indifference, seeing what was taking place in her classroom and ignoring him at the same time.

He woke up and the lights were off. Lunch. Mrs. Malseed was the only other body in the room, a faint orange light on at her desk creating a glow, she was eating a sandwich and flipping through a stack of papers.

He lifted his head in slow motion. "What time is it?"

"Oh Jesus. You're still here." She stood up with a jerk. "We've got to get you somewhere."

"Somewhere?"

"Well. Somewhere else."

She sent him home with a note that said he should get more sleep. His mother was worried.

After that, he resolved to read the book in class. He let it slip into the fold of his textbook, hoping to appear studious.

"Walter!" Malseed shoved the wrinkles of her face into his private world. "Walter, answer the question."

He looked to the invasion of her hideous features, dangerously close to him, emerging from the dream of his reading. "What?"

She snatched away the book, the page his thumb had rested over tearing and remaining underneath his palm while she shook the rest of the paperback savagely in his face. "You're reading? *In class?*"

For a moment, he thought she was about to spit on him.

The book went in the trashcan before he could blink at her.

■ ■ ■

When he got home that day, he looked through the house until he found her, by smell, half lying on the floor, her shoulders and neck propped up by the wall. There was a glass in her hand, or her hand was sloppily arranged around the glass which stood next to her, empty except for a liquid drop swishing at the bottom. She appeared, at least, settled in this position.

"Hey Mom."

"Yeah."

"Can we go to the library?"

"Get your homework done."

"I already did it."

"What time is it?"

"Can we go?"

"Give me a minute." He hovered, waiting. "A minute *alone.*"

He scurried from the bathroom. Though she hadn't looked capable of moving, the door slammed behind him.

He banged on it five minutes later and put his ear to the door in ten more minutes and heard a sound that might have been retching or a muffled response. He heard the eruption of shower water slapping the bathroom tiles.

He waited.

She had gotten him a library card at some point, never used, and he didn't use it now—reading the entirety of a tattered, worn library copy of *Brave New World* at the comfort of the library couch, homey and orange and gentle underneath him, the solitude of the place welcoming him. There was almost no one there except a librarian who ignored him behind the stereotypical, iconic thickness of her glass lenses. Thick enough to block out sight itself, who could see behind such a heavy layer of fog?

He stretched the book before him, devouring the pages. The cover was beaten. The public, entering and reentering the library, lusted for destruction, for malicious abuse, hardly reading, more like gnawing the books to pieces. By the last page, his mother stood behind him, the shadow of her on him, and he did not turn from the last paragraph, reading the sentences again and again.

"Let's go."

"One minute." He read the paragraph one more time, unwilling to pry himself from the spell, feeling the power, the repetition of the final words bouncing around inside him, how wonderful this was, how horrible that he existed outside of the world that he had uncovered inside here, what a nightmare life was.

"Okay," he announced at last, ready to return, his clothes dragging him back a little as he stood from the couch.

He went home, feeling satisfied as though something had at last been completed.

Stepping into what was next.

A friend.

Her name was Alice. She had been held back a grade, a little bit older. Heavyset, pimpled, her face hideous, raw, untreated, a wilderness of unforgiving, red mountain-scape, daring an adventurous explorer to risk traversing the land. The boys called her Ugly Alice, not just for cruelty's sake but to distinguish her from the other Alice in class with crystal blue eyes, her angelic white shoulder blades left uncovered by whatever she wore, spring or winter, the erotic straps of her dress displaying them.

That Alice would never bat an eye his way.

But at least Ugly Alice gave him the attention his misery had demanded—at last, he had found someone with the ability to notice him.

In the morning, sitting at his desk, Walter could blink and leave his eyes shut for twice as long as a usual blink, erasing the world around him for as long as his eyes were closed, and the dreams from the night before lingered into the day, as if he were still inside them, powerless to stop them from overtaking him, observing his inner mind's defiance of his supposed wakefulness, a coup against his consciousness, fighting to blink him back to sleep.

"My birthday is this Friday," Ugly Alice said, touching him with a pudgy thumb, whispering in the fragile soundlessness of another Tuesday, the class dead with the haze of morning time. He could feel the heat of her breath on his ear. This gooey whoosh of warm air startled him from his sleepy state.

"Oh really?" he said, opening his eyes.

"Are you coming to my birthday party?"

"Uh—"

"The party is this Friday." Her thumb was still touching him, he realized, looking down at the pink fatness, marveling at her touch, almost with horror. "My house. Be there or be a square."

He had never been to a girl's house—not even one his peers considered ugly. There was an allure to this, the prospect both scared and excited him, her offer's consequences sinking into his brain.

He prepared himself, entering a heavy pair of his man-jeans, taking counsel with his rap tape cassette for seven minutes of songs, listening closely for any advice he might've missed before.

But she was homely, no part of him responded to the femininity of her, he couldn't make himself like her. She didn't touch the memory of Kat and her grey eyes on him, her hand on his shoulder, her legs nodding to him underneath the water.

His mother dropped him off though the place was near enough to walk, and he sat inside, *inside* a girl's house, on the couch in her living room, Alice's mother serving him ice water.

He stared at his feet and the pattern of the rug. The color reminded him of the stained glass windows from a church, sharp red triangles that spiraled into thousands of sudden colors, though they all managed to have a neutral, related mood, pink then green, purple then orange.

"Where is everyone else?"

"I don't know," said Alice. "They'll be here later probably." She sat next to him at the couch, sipping at fruit juice, a deep, red shade of blood. He had turned down the juice when her mother offered it to him.

"When?"

"We're going upstairs now," she said, tugging him. He felt her mother's presence in the kitchen, drenched in the sound of running water and the humming of old radio songs.

Alice's room was only vaguely a girl's room. Mostly thick with boy-like things, blues and greens and a baseball bat and even a Nintendo tucked in the corner, not hooked up to a television.

She was unraveling a ratty plastic bag. A scent, potent as poison, came from the undone bag.

"Have you ever tried *this* before?"

"What is it?"

"I got it from my mom's boyfriend, Harry. You're going to *love* it. It is so much fun."

She retrieved the tool by which the drug would enter their bodies, a transparent, orange glasswork.

They set to work at their child-minds with these tools.

Here, another element to the boy's journey was allotted to him, one that could allow the restrained part of him to flutter free, drifting away without weight. The brain cells nudged at him before they went. Until this moment, he had felt undiscovered, hidden, alien, mostly unhappy.

Later on he would know—once the feeling had left him in a few hours—some part of him would spend the rest of its life secretly waiting for the feeling to come again.

The poison was now nestled deep, unable to be forced out by will or anything he could muster. And he did try to fight, not because he wanted it to leave, but at the delight of discovering how deliciously unable he was to do so, and how this only caused the feeling to grow stronger at the attempt. Pumping through his body, filling him.

He laughed and coughed and coughed and laughed.

"I do like this feeling," Walter told Alice, told himself, told no one, told the darkness that stretched around him that he had decided *could* be his friend.

"It is a perfect feeling," a voice said. Was the voice Alice's? There were hands on him. Hands on him. Pink, wet hands.

He looked down and felt that he was gripped tight by her. His pants were unzipped, one of her hands shoved in past her chubby wrist. Her other hand was on his shoulder, pinning him down. He was soft in her cold, freezing clutch. She was all over him, he imagined she was slobbering, a clownish smile on her face.

Before they got high, she had been sitting across the room from him and he wondered how so many physical, important things had happened without his noticing.

"No, no, no, no." He felt himself growing hard, nearly against his will. He resisted inside, helpless. She yanked at him but this was more painful than anything else.

"What's the matter?" she whispered, attempting to be soothing but her voice sounded cartoonish. The thoughts in his head whooshed over him, imperceptible despite being the one thinking them, he could not have told you what they were at all.

"No."

"Just relax."

At last he closed his eyes. He gave in; he might as well, all was pointless. Life. Her. This. Nothing had come to anything. He tried to focus in the dark of his shut eyes, but clarity eluded him even here. Her palm moved against him with rhythm, having turned warm against his skin, but he wasn't conscious of her there, only the motion of her. He felt something far away but still a part of him turn itself inside out. He opened his eyes and looked down. He had come, he looked down admiring himself a little for what had happened, proud as if this were some sort of accomplishment. Something he had been unable to do by himself and he *had* tried.

Then she was on him, her lips primed to swallow him. He could smell the grease on her pimples.

He shook from his daydream, he gained his senses just the right amount.

"What are you doing to me?" He pushed her off of him. "You drugged me!" he shouted, as if what had just happened a moment ago he had not regarded secretly as one of the greatest sensations ever to pass through him.

"I didn't mean anything by it. I didn't mean anything to be weird." Her lower lip tucked out. He looked at her and was disgusted.

He stood up and his pants fell down, he pulled them up and zipped them and held them there. His head spun, frustrated and nervous. He made to leave. He felt the uncomfortable wetness of himself beneath his jeans, squishing against his thighs as he moved.

"Wait. Walt!"

He darted from the room. His feet pounded on the stairs. He could feel the blood churning through his veins, the marijuana strong in him, his organs bouncing in his body in rapid movement like a seizure.

"What is the matter?" he heard or imagined he heard floating from the kitchen. He was in too much of a hurry to confirm the existence of this third party.

Back outside, at least safe, away from the strange form of harm that had made a move on him, his brain pounded at his forehead as if about to ooze through his face until it escaped him. Everything was awful again. At least he knew where he was, what neighborhood. He walked home, two miles, head down.

Outside was darkening by the time he returned, the house grey as rainwater. His mother, utterly unrelated to him, was crying. Her form slumped in a kitchen chair, a glass of her toxin before her on the table, mascara streaking her face like smears of muddy paint. He went right to his room and to bed without dinner inside of him.

He was asleep quickly, awake suddenly. He felt a hand on his blanketed stomach.

"My little boy," she whispered over him. "Still my little boy."

He did not open his eyes.

When the mundane, book-fed weekend reared its head and fell over dead, he spent the night before Monday, awake, dreading when he would have to be near Alice again for school. Images of Alice's heavy body hovered over him. Somewhere in the future. He was twiddling his thumbs next to her, a need to escape her presence wedged into his consciousness.

The next day, her desk was empty. The one next to his. He reached out to smack away a spider, pointlessly.

"Where's Alice?" he asked the teacher after class was over, almost hoping the answer to be that she was dead.

"She's not joining us today."

"What about tomorrow?"

"She's not joining us tomorrow."

"What happened to her?"

The teacher looked from Walter, shifting her attention, emotionless. "It's a delicate situation."

When he asked his mother, who knew Alice's mother vaguely, she looked at him and said, unmotherly and flat, "She's in the

Loony Bin. She tried to off herself."

"Oh," he said.

He was not shocked or startled. He had considered the same himself. Once or twice—in the piercingly stagnant moments before shut eyes turned to sleep—he fantasized a world without him in it, without his annoying consciousness pounding at his mind. The key word—fantasize. His life was a soft, uneventful thing; suicide existed only as fantasy.

How then could suicide be permitted to happen to anyone he knew, even an unsuccessful one?

He felt the transition of moving into a more serious life, where this was how things went. He felt that everything was different, that was all. Different in a way that was insignificant, like the color of something, anything, a trinket, a coffee mug, changing randomly to purple. He noticed this from the outside. He woke up in a different bed, in a different house, with a mother that had changed— without feeling the need to let him know the change had happened. Changed her hair, changed her drinking, changed the tone in which she spoke to her son. Changed the route of her nighttime explorations through the house.

But he failed to notice that he had changed as well. He read now with an intensity that casually set aside all other things. He read every book in the house with a title that tugged him toward it. His mother did not read much; most books were passed down from his grandmother. They littered the house, debris his mother had forgotten, waiting his discovery.

He had worked his way through the sprinkling of ancient, discarded soft covers, tears at the edges of the pages so gentle like someone had rubbed them with their palm until they disappeared. When they were read, he went looking for new books, stuffing his defeated mother into the driver's seat of the car and waiting for their arrival at the library.

He wore out his library card, until it too was falling apart like the old books, but more like a shard of glass would break, a crack running down the plastic that he fought to hold together. Finally he had to replace it. Five dollars—more than a day of lunch money, and worth it.

⁂

The groundhog had or hadn't discovered his shadow. Spring was headed his way, inevitable as trying to shake the will to survive. The girls' wear turned to shorts, skirts, flowerful things that seemed light and airy, almost empty inside, except that Walter knew the truth—they were full and that was the point.

He tried to wipe out the noise of spring with his reading. He was in the school cafeteria, alone with his book, placed before him, opened. He looked into the novel, through it, sentences, words, letters carrying him. He stopped reading long enough to notice the not too terribly urgent need to defecate. He stood up, bringing his book and leaving the tray of food behind at the empty football field of a table.

He entered the restroom, his sight dull with the watching of words, yellowish fluorescent lighting bright on his vision. He blinked, went for a stall, released himself from his bagging pants, dressed the seat in a protective layer of toilet paper.

He sat and waited. He pulled the book back in front of his face.

In a terribly sudden moment the lights of the restroom went out. He dropped his book, startled. He could still see faintly.

Beneath the door of his stall, he glimpsed the tumbling movement of a four-footed creature, a shadowed group of tennis shoes and hairless, daintier feet in flip flops, moving into the stall next to his. The toes were painted.

They were not quiet. The sound they made in their collaboration was a dishonorable tangle of heavy breath and sharp, feminine moans. He waited, sitting there afraid, wanting the yellow light to fill the room again and save him.

Five minutes passed. His eyes had adjusted to the dark and he thought about reading the book again, but he left it at his feet.

Curiosity overcame him, tiptoeing with stealth into his head.

He slid from the toilet seat and squatted slowly, his enormous pants still bunched at his ankles like a small creature curling up to sleep around his feet. He carefully inserted his head between the nasty, wet bathroom floor and the slightly raised wall of the stall. He could see the glimmer of long, naked girl legs that jerked with each breath and the bag of jeans entwined in them. He stuffed more of himself into the crack—nearly sticking there and feeling his hair smear with the wet of the floor—and looked up and saw the eyeballs, this time not calm but vibrating in their sockets.

They paused in their pleasure and turned to him, and he watched recognition form in them.

The eyes were grey.

CHAPTER II

From the City to the Beach

His face urine smeared. His heart not there when he went inside of himself to look for it. He closed the book he was reading and heard the cover slam shut, a sound that seemed as final and pronounced as if possessing the weight of an anvil, as if the sound represented finality this particular time. The shut book dug deep into his book bag, burrowing, making itself forgotten, entering hibernation. *Do Androids Dream of Electric Sheep?* He would read the final fifty pages years later, by the time he was almost a man, randomly coming across it again: the book could not be held back. A thin, flimsy library book, never in a library again, handled and handled until all but the ink on the inside pages had nearly faded, the ink letters still clear as day on the page, like the ink was indestructible and Walter could burn the book and the letters would hover in the air, black, bold, unkillable.

"What's wrong with you?" his mother asked him. She was in nothing but a ragged brown shirt and gym shorts and Walter felt the queasy threat of her figure, scantily camouflaged underneath the worn costume, littered with holes, strings of dangling yarn.

He turned away from the veiny, poorly maintained, nearly forty-year-old body that he had emerged from fourteen years ago.

"Dad."

"Dad what?"

"Dad."

Instead of responding, she made a gargling sound in her mouth, a broken water pipe, the main busted, no longer doing what it was supposed to be doing, spewing water through holes.

"*Dad.*" He spoke demanding this time, his voice a post holding the word up.

She snatched Walter's hand from his arm, clutching hard

enough that the threat of violence hovered, except that Walter's expression refuted the possibility, calm, empty and unafraid. She had a pen in her hand, she was inking numbers into his palm. He looked down at her work and tugged his hand back the instant he counted ten digits.

He went to the phone furthest away from her smell.

"Hello?"

"Dad."

"Walt?"

"Dad."

"Walter! How are you doing?"

"Fine." There was no question in his tone, firmness beyond his years.

"What's going on? How is school?"

The last time they had talked, one month and two weeks. Merry Christmas, sorry I'm not there. The last time his father had physically introduced himself into the world Walter existed in. One year and a half plus some days and hours. The father left the mother and her son, guiltily, not unknowing of the reeling, gaping hole in the earth that would unsurface their hearts, replacing them, sucking up every other part of them. Except for their minds, leaving them behind in the real world, suffering in the detailed consciousness of everything around.

"Fine. School's fine. Dad—"

How does he ask? What are the words that will save him from the wreckage of his future?

"Yeah?"

"Dad, I—" He felt the need to compose the words first in his head, to craft them with magic, to save himself with words somehow.

"What is it, Walter?"

"Let me live with you."

They came finally, but the moment he spoke them it seemed as though he had walked into a dream. From here, anything could happen to him.

*　*　*

Walter imagined the beach. He had never been to the one where his father lived, he saw it as locked away from every other beach, a secret beach, powerful in this secretness, ancient, maybe the beach where Noah landed. Scattering and confusion of the animals as they went to repopulate the earth. A beach where all things started, Wrightsville Beach, his toes would curl into the sand, and then he would walk to the edge where the world turned to water forever. The water falling in between his toes and the salt changing his pores. The three and a half hairs sprouting from his big toe pulled at by the soft but inevitable tug of the current. Swimming, hiccups of salt carrying him.

He packed his young life into three cardboard liquor boxes. Or four? Later he had a feeling four but he lost one of them along the way, or his mother lost it, almost on purpose, hoarding part of him away for herself, fighting to keep whatever she could, though he knew she didn't want him there, couldn't have him there anymore.

His father came to pick him up in a car he had never seen, but he only vaguely noticed cars, a trash color red, large in the most inconvenient sense.

His father was barely recognizable.

There were features left there that a year's absence or thirty years absence could not erase, the beach could not snatch the wrinkles at the corner of his mouth that teased at a frown or an ambiguous smile, could not scratch the surface of his aged dignity, preserved by the adultness of him, infinite to Walter, an abyss he glimpsed in the depth of his father's eyes, a power greater than him, like having to look away from the sun or being conquered by its vastness.

But the greyness to his hair had turned blond with sunshine. The complexion of his skin had a new glow. Walter thought of radioactivity and skin cancer.

From the city to the beach.

Away from one of the only true cities in North Carolina, the downtown heart with building after building snatched from an imagined New York by southerners, stolen in their dreams. To the windy, empty, undiscovered, small beach town, with swinging signs and teenagers and almost as high rent that continued to grow higher as the tourists circled, hungry for another place to waste time.

One of the boxes had his Super Nintendo and he didn't know which one. He rode in the backseat, a hand on the box he could reach, guarding it with the firm positioning he had assumed, feeling the cardboard underneath his fingertips, stoic and still as a statue, immobile, afraid that the rocking of the car could affect the fragile circuitry inside the little machine.

He looked out the window on a dare to himself, taking his hands from the boxes just long enough to shove his face out of the rolled down window, to watch the yellow dashes, the infinitely long white line swallowed by the cars pressing forward, hungrily enveloped by the journey he was on, but still more white lines up ahead, forever stretching into the future, never-ending, continuing, not caring how long he had traveled before.

You will never make progress, the road insisted.

The house—painted puke green and shuttered up—was several miles from the water. The road was gravel and when car tires went over it, the rocks made that crunchy sound like how eating cereal sounds deafening to the person eating it.

"Hi Walter!" A chirp, a hiccup, a voice too young, too accidental to say anything on purpose. A voice that sounded almost younger than his. "I've heard about you! My name is Teresa."

He examined her, her face small and bright and the proportions of her smile too large to fit, noticing with some discomfort that he was attracted to her; he was almost fifteen now and attraction to women was something he had to deal with despite that they existed in a world he had no access to.

She was wearing a shirt, obviously one of his father's. Almost playing a joke by how unselfconscious and seductive she was in it.

All his stuff was tucked into shelf and closet in minutes and then Walter was spread out on his new bed and his eyes were closed and he felt so utterly conscious of the cotton of his clothes running over his skin and rubbing him that he started to remove his shirt then stopped, halfway done, his shirt halfway off and his new bed under him and him beneath the clothes, feeling everything suddenly as alien. His body still, his eyes closed, his mind pounded at his head, demanding answers for what he had done, why he was here, like his brain had been drugged and held captive in his body, waking up here and only now realizing something was different.

What was he doing here?

And with that Walter entered another phase of his existence, the first one that had been orchestrated by him. His perception seemed to ready itself, moving into a fighting stance, every aspect of him suspect of the new life.

After all, things had been too odd for too long.

The time was eight at night. Eventually he fell into something like sleep on the bed, clothes on, only asleep enough that he could remain somewhat aware of the alien surroundings, the freshness not to be trusted. Cognizance not allowing him to entirely turn his back yet, not allowing him to go into the real sort of sleep that would repair him, the kind where he would forget where he was, falling down a bottomless hole.

Of course, his father looking in on him at some unknown point, his heavy, adult presence behind him, peeking at him through the blur of his half consciousness, a peek, a gentle nudge behind him, almost unfelt, delicate, so thin and flimsy and almost not there at all.

* * *

Two a.m. He opened his eyes. He was awake, like he saw everything in his new room through a clear lens that revealed all the intricacies and angles normally invisible. In the dark, he could observe better. He sat up from the bed, feeling free from the sleep that had softly kidnapped him, then, not explaining itself, set him loose again.

He looked back at the grey creases and wrinkles of his bed sheets and the folded quilt on top and the two pillows, a landscape of cotton and comfort, although hollowed and abandoned the instant he awoke.

He moved from the bed and realized not only were his clothes still on but his shoes were as well. He started to slide his socked feet from them, then decided not to when he realized the laces were so tight he would have to untie them if he wanted to take them off.

He wandered into the kitchen, almost by mistake, walking through the house, discovering things and details he would never have noticed in the light.

With his father asleep, he felt how barren the house was.

He could just feel the presence of someone, but not quite, and when he turned around and saw there was no one there, he felt unsatisfied, as if there was a person he could not see. The emptiness had grown and was itself an invisible person, silently judging him, watching him with no fear of being detected.

He started to open drawers in the kitchen cabinets, rummaging, pillaging in the dark, running from any thoughts that flashed through his head and asked him, calmly, *What are you doing? Why are you here?*

The thought spiraled, he slipped away, palming silverware and kitchen towels, touching some paper wrapped in slick shredded cellophane, plastic, something that might have been what he was searching for, although by touch could be a piece of trash. Ripping it from the drawer, he held the discovery in front of his face.

A pack of Camel cigarettes.

He sat on the porch in the clearness of the night sky, no stars, no headlights, no bright neighbor's windows. He heard maybe the drunken call of older boys wandering the streets, or a dog barking. They did not matter. They did not invade his new silence.

The first time he smoked a cigarette.

He fired up the plastic lighter his father would use for charcoal in the grill, another trinket Walter had retrieved from the kitchen drawers. He drew a deep breath as the tip glowed orange. He wasn't sure *how* to smoke, *how* to inhale, *how* to use the cigarette as a filter to breathe through, and then he was smoking just a moment after trying. He did not cough.

He went inside his new self, a little bit tougher; the cigarette had attacked him and he emerged from the assault more alive and unconquered. He watched the cigarette shrink into the filter as he puffed. He felt the nicotine beat at his brain, an organic heart placed inside of him, separate but doing something to the rhythm of his body. He watched the smoke float and drift from his mouth, breath transformed into clouds, poisonous wisps that swam through the dark, faint lives fading almost the instant they began.

The noise of boys' mischief echoed in the black air. He listened as the sounds grew closer, voices bouncing like the conversation was a red ball tossed back and forth between them, like they were trading voices and this was an established game with rules. Walter felt their boyish voices almost on him, circling him, he could see a snapshot of their faces passing across the street in their clumsy, unpracticed march. The dull yellow streetlight made their five faces glow for an instant, in this moment of revelation their faces chattered, unaware of Walter's presence, except for one that met his smoky stare in a broken second.

Walter studied the boy's manlike face under the streetlight, turning the second into a frozen hour in his mind, destroying time, turning it infinite for as long as he could.

The boy looking back at him, recognizing Walter was familiar to him, recognizing Walter as a part of the background, something that was supposed to be there and nothing even unexpected or surprising.

The boy had a light mustache, pubic hairs plucked from his groin and applied to his face. His expression was dreadful, deadpan.

But also sort of ironic, gloating. The boy to his left laughed and he looked on, a thousand years older.

When they were gone, Walter put out his cigarette in a glass of water on the rusty bistro table beside him. The cigarette hissed at him, angry at the end of its life. He poured the ashy water into the large green trash can in the front yard. He carried the glass back inside with him, a hand on his stomach, marveling at the ease with which he had survived the experience. His insides tickled, giddy with the success of his experiment, impressed with his maintained secrecy. As of that moment he was the only one who knew what had taken place. He slipped the pack of Camels back in the drawer where he had found them, patting them like a companion, arranging them precisely how he imagined they had been positioned in the drawer when he discovered them.

He still did not cough. Impressed with himself, he breathed normally, perhaps better than before, as if the smoke had reached inside of him and cleaned him out. He went to the fridge, opened the door, felt the dull light softly nuzzling him, yellow, gentle. He pulled out a carton of milk and poured himself a glass, without quite realizing he was using the glass that had been on the porch. Oh well, he thought, drinking it, gulping it, feeling the liquid churn cool and white inside of him, clearing out his insides, turning everything inside of him to magic—the feeling wonderful, perfect. He could live for a hundred years off this milk. He gulped faster, the sooner he could put the stuff in him, the more powerful the effect would be.

He looked at the clock on the wall. Four. He was aware that his father might be up soon, might find him, might even smell the smoke on his clothes. He thought about this almost long enough to care and then he stopped thinking about it. This was how he would live his life from now on, he thought, he would not care.

The living room now.

He turned on the television and the bustled, colorful confusion filled the screen. He mashed the volume button down,

down, quieting the chatter into a calming, fizzling pleasantness. He changed the channels until they turned grey and fuzzy and sizzling. He paused, considering this, then continued to change the channels.

He turned to a channel where the outline of bodies could be traced in the mountain of towering silver fizz. Despite himself, a tumbling excitement beat at his chest and his fingers twitched, hovering over his pants.

He did not sleep.

But by morning he was in a space where his awareness had glided away, so that he did not notice his father turning on the lights.

"Walter."

Where was he? Whose voice said his name like that, so familiar, so intimate, but irritated too?

"Walter?"

He tried to shake himself of the spell he had entered. He moved his hand, put his pants back together. He recognized the slowness of the movement traveling through him, he throbbed, the throbbing trickling down his body, the ache of not enough sleep and not enough time spent regrouping from life.

"Son."

He looked up to his father, standing in front of him, or had he been standing in front of him before? His father, a short man even through fourteen-year-old eyes, still towering now, still looming, judging, his old, tan lip twitching in dangerous thought. His forehead wrinkled appearing to have been removed from his skull and squeezed back on, crooked, sloppily shoved over the skeleton and the brain.

"What are you doing?"

The boy started to move a little, shaking his head, preparing to get up, but then he stayed on the couch. He opened his mouth but his voice felt stolen, left behind somewhere. Words scratched at the surface, struggling, drowning in the water of his throat.

His father raised a hand. "No. Don't say anything. Just—from now on—don't stay up so late. Summer or not, you need to sleep some."

After this was delivered, his father's hovering over him grew awkward. They both waited for something, watching each other, existing in a tender state of cease fire.

His father lifted the wallet from his pocket and tossed a ten dollar bill next to Walter. The bill waited to be picked up in the crease of the couch, wrinkled and folded, a failure at origami, some intricate detailed something, but possibly a piece of balled up trash.

"Just do something. Go to the beach. Get ice cream for God's sakes. It's the summer Walter."

Walter looked at the money uncrinkling from his father's fist. He stared down at it in a vague way, like he was from a place where money had not yet been introduced.

When he finally looked up, he was the only one in the room. He pocketed the bill. He stood from the sofa, rediscovering his legs. He looked out the window, the ugly red colored car missing from the driveway.

His father had left him with ten dollars and an awkward moment.

There was another car in the driveway that he had not noticed the night before, yellow, faded, dusty.

The woman was here?

No. Not a woman, a girl, an older girl, not close to his age, but close enough, close enough that in his fantasy he could almost touch her form with the invisible tentacles that sprouted from the male part of him.

Teresa was her name.

It was morning, was she asleep still? He could look in on her.

He undid his laces and took off his shoes, at long last. His feet throbbed faintly—released. He tip-toed behind the stealth of his socks, softly reaching the door to his father's bedroom. The house had three bedrooms and one was empty, already open a peek, seeming to invite him. If it wasn't closed why shouldn't he open it? Why shouldn't he gently push it just a little further open, just enough that he could see inside—

Perhaps he could glimpse her body, or at least the outline under one of his father's shirts, pretending to protect its elegance, but really just reminding him of what was there, that she was a woman or a girl with a body like a bottle, a perfect body, a body crafted to call to him, to call his horrifically young and painful and unsatisfied youth, the ache in him, the itch.

He pushed the door an inch and heard a terrific creak, a squeal of wood, and heard or thought or imagined a feminine groan, a soft hint of life, a dream, an accidental sound, a woman's voice alive in the room. He recoiled.

He shrunk from the door, terrified. Had he made a mistake that would cost the life of another? The death his fault and he would always, always know that he had been the cause, responsible for this loss of human life.

He took off his socks and slapped sandals to his feet in a move to escape before the death took place and everyone knew the blood was on his hands and his fault, even now he imagined he heard her coming to in soft, elegant moans, like attempting to speak under anesthesia, the suggestion of language under the inarticulate whimpers he imagined he heard drifting from the room through the wider crack in the door. He thought he heard her say his father's name.

"Sam."

He had.

"Sam."

There was no mistaking it now. She was awake. The damage had been done.

"Sam, what time is it?"

Walter scurried off, tumbling his way through the house and out the front door, trampling down the driveway in his rubber sandals, the loose Velcro straps slapping his feet and the pavement, feet then pavement.

He hit the road, slowing. The sun was oppressive, infinite, taking over the sky like an enemy, vanquishing its emptiness. Sunlight was in his eyes as he walked and he rubbed at them. He bent over to tighten the strap on his sandal.

The beach houses passed around him in blurry motion—bright green, baby blue, even pink, some of the houses on stilts as if able to walk, the colors of the world turned happier and happier in the daylight, his mood shifting slightly. Anything was possible here.

His nose led him to the beach, salt drifting through the air and into his body through his breath and tugging him along, absorbing him.

He moved with no plan, a natural motion, the progression of an animal moving towards food; he had not set out to walk to the beach. But suddenly he felt sand grains rolling down the crack in his sandal, digging their way into his skin, burying themselves in the soles of his feet, the smallest rocks, burrowing. He looked up and saw that the sun had erupted around him, climaxing, reaching a peak unthinkable before. How could the sun increase in brightness, in power? How could this sun be the same as the one from yesterday, some dull orange globe that faded in the sky?

He thought that everything below would wilt, would grow flimsy, withering into air until even that was gone. The sun would suck up everything, ending all things.

A sound, soft and loud at the same time—the water touching the shore over and over and over.

He felt the motion of the sea before witnessing the salty white-blue mass, that methodical in and out flow massaging his mind sweetly, relieving the tension of that horrible sun, a deep sleep moving over his brain. He closed his eyes and listened.

Summer, summer, hot summer, nature sizzling over it like raw red meat quickly turning black on the grill.

Sand stretched to his left and right, hot yellow peppered in the pink of bodies.

A seagull—something papery and not edible in its mouth that looked from a trashcan—eyed him inquisitively. Asking the only question the seagull was capable of asking: Feed me?

He removed his sandals and his shirt and tucked them under a bench. On the bench, he saw an expletive carved, deep as a hideous scar, sloppily etched into the wood. He took a moment to consider its blasphemous author.

He rolled up his jeans and moved to the water, still not quite looking at it. He stood right where he knew the water would reach, the sand like clean mud under his feet, and he waited for the water to touch his skin, to come back to him.

His jeans slightly wet—the feeling not at all unpleasant, but beautiful, perfect. He reached into his pocket to remind himself that the ten dollar bill was still there and he started walking along the shoreline, salt water passing over him and then retreating and then passing over him again as he walked.

A group of four or five teenaged girls walked by, a few feet from him, wearing their young bodies open, explicit, as if they had picked them to match their colorful bikinis rather than the other way around. Only one was fat and even she was comfortable in the weight of herself, the movement of her body, natural and powerful, daring Walter to not notice.

There was one in a bikini colored Easter egg green, the palest but still more tan than the paper whiteness of his chest, she turned towards him as they walked by him and she smiled and said, "Hi!"

Her tone was almost suggestive, something attached he could not read.

He had walked past them before he realized he had not said a word back, not even looked back at her, other than a quick glimpse in her direction, only long enough to remember what she looked like forever, for the rest of his life.

How had she even noticed him?

His pale, diseased skin didn't even match across its own landscape. His face red, his chest paper, his arms a cardboard color.

He hadn't realized there were people here, not quite a hundred, but maybe a hundred, maybe very close to a hundred. Probably almost exactly one hundred people, half of them girls his age or close enough to his age.

They sprouted all around him, materializing at a merciless pace, and rapidly there were more than a hundred, maybe thousands? He had no sense of things such as this.

There were girls on every side of him, appearing right beneath him. He moved more carefully, afraid he might step on one. Skin. Skin. Skin taking over the world, tan, brown, healthy, golden, glowing. No one was as pale as he and they all flaunted this. The giggles of the girls swarmed from all sides, were they laughing at him? Were they laughing at the color of him?

He hung his head and kept going.

▧ ▧ ▧

He had no idea how long he traveled along the shoreline. He had turned around, reversing direction at least three times. It could have been thirty minutes or three hours. Enough time that he was sunburnt. He could feel the top of his skin transform, separate from the rest of his body, then die and become something different. He had some idea that he was searching for the girl in the green bikini. She would remember him.

He imagined he saw her in another group of girls approaching, but they were tramps, mock royalty in their boyish saunter, the heavy nature of their stompish walk, the way they shoved their nearly naked, tan bodies at him with no carefulness, no modesty.

Could this be the same gang, just that they had changed a little with the afternoon? Gaining confidence, losing innocence, growing up in the space of an hour? They were taller, more beautiful, but uglier too in their defiance and their angry, noisy chatter. They seemed to be arguing with themselves—or no, a single organism, they argued against everything else, defying everyone.

The most tan one wore a green bikini, dark green, forest green, not the girl he searched for but close enough for now. She had a scowl when he looked at her though, ready to meet him, prepared. Her face was still desirable in agitation, but not pretty anymore, projecting hate onto him, maybe misguided, but focused on him. She could have been fourteen, fifteen, sixteen, seventeen. But her hate was a million years old.

He had to talk to her now, he had been looking for her, even if it wasn't exactly her, in a way it was, to his memory.

What should he say?

"Hey. I have ten dollars." He crumpled and uncrumpled the bill, one hand in his jean pocket.

"Fuck off."

The moment she spoke to him, hate passed through her and her expression went neutral, like he was not there and she looked right past him, not speaking to him at all, talking through him and sauntering on, sashaying off coolly, the tension released once he had spoken and proven himself no threat to her, not even the mildest bit of danger to her in his pipsqueak of an attempt to draw her to him, to acknowledge her.

He felt miniscule, erased, he stopped dead in his tracks and turned to watch them as they kept on walking like large animals at the top of the food chain. Right past him, prey not worthy of the hunt, not enough of his scrawny, skeletal pale sickliness to be divvied up between them. He watched their asses, swaying in colorful bikini bottoms, the rhythm, the pattern to their walk, this part of them ignoring him as much as the rest of them, sunlight a white blinding glare along the curve of the forest green of one hump. He kept watching until they were out of sight, motionless, felt the sting of his lust, and the deepness of the hole inside of him, going on forever.

He started walking again, in the direction he imagined was homeward, even though he was clueless at this point, he walked faster, faster, barely not running, thoughts thinking through him, girls rising around him, closing in and suffocating him.

Was there a girl anywhere who remembered what he looked like? He wondered if they too thought about him, if there were girls who desired him, who remembered him from a long time ago, maybe from another life he had lived, girls panting for him, drooling for him, hypnotized by the thought of him, his touch, it could paralyze them.

If he left them alone for a moment they would die.

He bought a milkshake from a food truck stepping onto pavement again. He handed the frowning man his ten dollar bill and the man handed him back five dollars and several coins.

His mouth sucked at the straw of his shake forcefully, the ice cream coming through with the ferocity of water tearing through a fire hose.

He put it in the trash can and set out to make his way home.

Even on the street there were still girls rising around him, unavoidable. He felt the humiliation that had blemished his spirit now fade and he grew hopeful again, thinking he saw the girl from before. She, at least, had met his gaze. But still not her: only two other girls with her and her bikini was not green, but speckled with flowers. She was not quite as pretty. He smiled at her and she smiled back.

This was enough.

"Hey."

"Hi there!" Her smile turned on him, questioning, unafraid but uncertain.

"I have ten dollars." Not realizing in the moment he didn't anymore.

"Do you now?" She giggled and the joyous, non-maliciousness of her tone sent the giggle through her two friends, repeated, wavelike in its motion through them. One had on sunglasses and her smile seemed the whiter for it, teeth shining, exposed.

"Why are you telling me?"

He chewed at his lip, struggling to think quick enough, fighting to think the exact right thought into his mind and to push it through his lips.

"Because it's enough for two ice creams."

She looked back at her two girlfriends, smiling at them, a secret smile, a communicative smile, reaching into them like language.

"Okay," she said.

She waved at her friends. They conspired to reconvene at the beach, at the water, at the pier.

She followed him back to the truck where he remembered he now only had five dollars.

He handed the incessantly frowning man back the bill in exchange for a three dollar sundae, a tower of white and streams of chocolate syrup, a lone cherry, which she plucked from the top as if the sole portion of the dessert she intended to eat, putting the cherry in her mouth so daintily, setting it aside in her cheek, the hump of skin tracing the circular shape until she swallowed and he heard the gulp, clear, watery, natural.

He watched her eat, hovering, admiring the gingerly motion to her eating, the careful nature, but unsure of his place, he hung at her side. The red plastic spoon moved in and out of her mouth, his eyes followed.

"You're not going to get any?"

His eyes darted to the ground. "No."

"Well," she tossed the plastic cup away, littering happily, "I'm going to go find my friends now. Bye!"

She scuttled off in the direction of the beach. He realized he didn't know what her name was.

Was there a girl anywhere who was willing to discover him?

Almost dark by the time he found the house. He wandered through the neighborhood for ages, near tears a few times, a part of him wishing for his mother to appear, a part of him believing she would. The sun had turned orange and safe, less demanding, retreating for a while to regain strength. The shadows had begun to stretch, growing, sneaking up on the land with a grey, cool touch.

He pushed the unlocked door open.

His father was there, wearing a suit and tie, ready to roar at him.

"Walter, where have you been all day? Where is your shirt?"

He looked to his chest, that bench far behind him, everything forgotten, left behind. He felt the floorboards under his sandy toes.

It had been a long day.

"I was about two minutes away from calling the police."

"Why are you dressed like this?" Walter asked, without thinking much about why the question had come, but naturally sensing something significant, something he wanted to know.

His father looked down at his wear as if only now noticing it. "I was wearing this all day. I spent today looking for jobs."

"You don't have a job?"

His father bent his head away from Walter, stomping off into the kitchen. "Well. I, I think I have one now. Probably. It's at a furniture store. I would be the store manager."

Walter yawned. "That's good."

"Sure. It's great. Have you had dinner?"

"I had a milkshake."

■ ■ ■

He looked at himself naked in the mirror, naked except for the tight, elastic Fruit of the Loom cupping his genitals almost spilling out. Handsome red demon. He was so sunburnt, when he touched any part of him it went to the whitest white, the shape his fingerprint left behind for a second. The redness of his body throbbed, but he imagined he looked good in the mirror, he imagined the color added to his body, powerful, glowing, invincible. He would change. He would become superheroic. He did not look bad. He looked good. He was certain, carefully inspecting himself, studying himself. He looked fine; there was nothing wrong with him, he recognized this now. Here he was in this body, this body put together by his life and by everything that happened to him. Now he could be allowed to become himself. Everything that hurt him could go away. The girls would love him now.

■ ■ ■

The beach drew him like flypaper. Stuck to the arsenic wax, he struggled to crane his head, to witness the girls, half-dressed and oblivious of his attention, parading flesh.

He found the girl in the flowered bikini again and waved more dollars of his father's money from his pocket. He asked her what her name was and she said Mary. His was Walter, he offered to buy her ice cream again, laughing, all a joke, all such a wonderful joke, this life that repeated itself, that ran in a circle, bringing them together again, her freckles standing out on her cheeks with the dignity of little toy soldiers, organized perfectly in lines, almost marching, the handsome organization of those freckles across her cheeks, he had not noticed them before and they colored her smile.

She did not smile at him really.

She let him buy her ice cream again. This time he had enough for himself too and purchased the same thing as her, another chocolate sundae, greedily scarfed down alongside her, unable to copy her dignity, this gentle calm of her eating like a skilled musician plucking at the instrument of her choice. She finished her sundae before him, her method somehow more efficient.

"What now?" he asked, looking up from the trash of his sundae, his lips smeared with chocolate, close enough to her that he could smell her, feel her little breathing. He dared to reach out and touch the top of her hand, smushing under one finger the little delicate vein that squirmed through into her knuckles. He was trembling.

"I'm going to go hang out with my friends at the pier." She looked down. "You can come . . . I guess."

His insides fell, the hope wiped away. "No thanks."

The next time he saw her walking across the street on her way to the beach he made no move to acknowledge her and she clearly saw him but did not as much as nod in his direction.

Mary.

He was at the beach, sulking in his new red bathing suit, the one his father got from the surf shop, a quarter of the summer already evaporated since he had moved here, his pockets empty except maybe for a drop of salty water and a few grains of sand, alone, walking along the orange fading heat of the beach, the day turning shadowy.

He saw them. Two boys. They looked older. They sat in awkward lawn chairs next to a cooler from which they pulled out beers. Once he had tasted beer from the slivery slosh left over at the bottom his mother's unfinished glass, giving into pure curiosity and being disgusted. Bubbling, spicy mud sizzling in his stomach turning against it. Cold, carbonated dirt.

He would have kept walking by them. But one of those boys he saw was the boy from the night he moved to Wrightsville, with the indifferent look and the faint but very manly mustache. Something drew him to the mustached child, something primordial, an empathy inherited from a former life perhaps. His indifferent gaze turned on Walter as Walter asked the two boys if he could have a beer. It was necessary to ask for a beer, of course he asked for a beer, he had to show them he could ask for a beer as casually as asking their names a heartbeat after they tossed a can in his direction, caught in one smooth motion as his hand shot out.

"Tyler," said the other one he hadn't seen before. Tyler was wearing a collared shirt with the top three buttons undone. It was plaid and stood out from his body like a cardboard cutout of a shirt held in front of his chest, rather than clothing wrapped around it.

"I don't have a name," said the mustached boy. He was a creepy, full grown man, and his leeriness loomed over Walter, indifferent. His lips parted like he was about to say something else but he didn't. He had a green, unsigned cast on one foot but no crutches.

"We call him Smiley," Tyler said. "What's your name Kid?"

"Walter."

"I don't *really* have a name," Smiley insisted. His clumsy words slid through his mouth this time, colliding into each other. He burped.

"Everybody calls him Smiley." Tyler shrugged.

Walter was afraid to ask how a boy could not have a name. He popped the can open and shook a drop into his mouth. It tasted horrible like muddy ice.

"Good beer," he said.

"Dude, whatever. It's PBR." Tyler chugged at least half a can after saying this. "We have liquor in here too if you want."

"Here," Smiley said, faintly sarcastic rather than his usual robotic tone. He handed Walter a water bottle. There was nothing to betray the camouflage of the contents, the liquid inside crystal clear.

"Go on. Drink it." Smiley showing his teeth now, his lips bent back, sinister, vicious in a display of predatory glee.

Walter unscrewed the cap and the smell hit him. The smell of his mother. He didn't want to drink the stuff at all. But—after a peek of fear at his watchful peers—he threw it back and wrapped his lips around the bottle, forced it into him, it flowed into him, a fire pouring inside, glorious pain, perfection.

As though he had opened his mouth underwater and realized he could breathe even though the experience was different.

He did not mind the sting, but he coughed, and they laughed at him a little.

They respected him suddenly. Tyler reached over and patted him on the back. Smiley stared on but the mocking nature fell from his mood.

"Chase it with your beer," Tyler said.

"I don't really like the beer." Walter handed the can back to him. He drank from the water bottle again, marveling at the beautiful pain. Tasteless and bitter at the same time, amazing. He held the bottle before him, fascinated, touching it. Already he felt the change moving in him, digging in, it would not be stopped now.

He drank again. This time he didn't stop for as long as he could, as an experiment, feeling the icy knife of the liquor squirm into his body. It cut his insides and he loved it. The first pain he ever felt that he truly loved.

"Easy dude," Tyler warned. "It's gonna hit you. Hard."

"What do you mean?"

Before Walter had pushed the question through his mouth, it hit him. The sky was darker, about to rain, the shadow stretching under him no longer belonged to him but to someone behind him that hid when he turned around. The sand was new under his feet, the texture different, special, astounding. He inspected a grain with his toe as carefully as if about to be attacked by the sand.

His senses seemed rearranged, not in their normal spots, and he could smell through his ears, see through his taste buds. He could drink vodka through his eyes.

Time passed. He drank from the water bottle on and off, now sitting in the sand next to Smiley and Tyler in their beach chairs. They burped and tossed beer cans into the sand.

Walter opened his mouth to drink more and found he could not verify his mouth was open, the sensation that it was there had disappeared.

The blue of the sky. The dull blue of the sky. The dull bluegrey rain clouds. Black. Black and flashes of light wedged in between and black.

"Smiley. Help me turn him over."

He was aware that sandy, slimy chunks were in his mouth, tasting of eggs. He felt warmth bubble through him and spill out, too much warmth to be contained, like his body had found perfection for a second but had to reject it since he was, after all, flawed. He felt inside out, he felt over full, he felt all wrong but still glowing.

"Like that?"

He was lying down. He was lying down? He was on his side now, maybe, being on his side had no meaning to him, not really a position, the only position existed at the center of his forehead, right behind the skin, there was his consciousness dimming and observing, everything else was outside of this tiny spot where he waited for things to make sense again, if they ever would.

"Yeah, that's good. So he won't choke. I mean, you know. Little shit dying on us."

He felt it coming again, traveling through him, awful nightmare of life, spilling out, slimy eggs squealing as they crawled upward, was he dying like Tyler had said? Who was Tyler? Had someone just said he was going to die? That would be better, that would be honorable, everything was out of him, he was entirely inside out. He shut his eyes.

"Let's go to the arcade."

"Yeah."

He wouldn't throw up anymore, he wouldn't. He had thrown up for the last time ever. He felt the beauty of this thought, the dignity of it freed him. He would never throw up again, there wasn't anything left to throw up.

He struggled to shut his eyes tighter. His head beat him into something that was not sleep and he knew it, sensed it, even as he felt it swallow him. Just black. Maybe he had died for a little while. Maybe he had.

Would he come back?

He had to come back, of course.

He woke up as soon as he had that thought, the thought itself waking him, his mind said to him plainly: No Walter. No, no, no. You aren't dead. That is ridiculous.

It was nighttime and he shivered, in nothing but his little red swim shorts. He smelled the vomit, still in him. He spat up the leftovers. He thought of standing but didn't. He waited to feel better, spitting but not throwing up anymore, not throwing up.

He stood at last and went into the sea, crouching, cold and shivering, washing himself off.

He knew that he had done a horribly dangerous thing.

He came home with his head hung.

His father at work, though it was late. He let himself in with the key under the doormat and went to the shower, defeated. Teresa was not there. The house rang hollow with his defeat.

He knew it had been dangerous. He couldn't end up like his mother, staying in a tower, life going on underneath. He could not let that happen to him, he knew instantly. That was impossible, he had a tingling creep under his skin, someone had handed him a video cassette including the moment of his death, and told him to watch it once a day for the rest of his life.

So he decided to not be drunk anymore.

Despite that it was the greatest feeling he had ever experienced.

CHAPTER III
The Witch

Summer ripped through Walter's life with the permanence of a mosquito snubbed out in a splatter of blood, dribbling down a bare shoulder. Walter and his father. And sometimes Teresa, his father's twenty-eight-year-old squeeze. In the beach bungalow they didn't even own, in a cluster at the dinner table, huddled around each other as if for warmth.

Life was as irritating to Walter as his lust, following the sway of teenage bikini buttocks before him at the beach, plump, round, neon and glistening in the sun, always ignorant of his attention.

Fifteen now. School came back to him, unwanted; he couldn't shake himself from its clutches—the looks on the faces of boys and girls who were supposed to be his age, the heat of them looking at his back, growing hot until he turned around, only to find the sensation behind him on the other side now. School and binders and notebooks and number two pencils and boys and girls shifting at their desks and the numbing tick of the clock and school. The return of it.

His father couldn't afford rent at the beach anymore, and they moved close to downtown, right where the city spilled into ancient churches, the red brick layers speaking their worth to him, every corner of the place a relic preserved in dust.

Walter's school district was now in downtown, the building split in half by the street with furious cars darting in between the school grounds, like a hive of angry bees in the middle of a house, oblivious, racing back and forth, vicious in their circling, but organized as well.

The catwalk, enclosed in cage, went high above the road between the two buildings and Walter watched the cars below in between his classes, thinking about nothing, wondering if he could force himself into the lives of his fellow students. They poured by him while he stood there, he as effective against the current of their lives as if he stood in the ocean, curling his toes into the muddy sand, digging in for some illusion of grip. Imagined control. His level of focus could never reverse the motion of the waves rushing over his feet.

The first day of school came. The second day and the third. Still, he was silent in his classes in the chaotic noise of his peers swirling about him.

What did he have to do to become one of them?

There was at least a single person Walter had a brief history with. Tyler was in his math class. He suspected Tyler shouldn't have been in any of his classes; he looked eighteenish and Walter always thought he lived at the beach, putting him probably in a different district. But there he was each day, at the desk, fingers drumming the desk, a metronome, rhythm moving forward, always proceeding.

Something was wrong with the world, Walter sensed and suspected, feeling a drop in that untouchable place inside of him, in charge of his intuition. The world refused to abide by the rules and its inhabitants were forced to wander about, leaderless. Anarchy.

Tyler. The older boy sat at the desk, three boys and a girl to Walter's left, drumming, waiting for the end of the day, waiting, waiting, a machine—meticulous in its design—constructed to wait, to sit and do nothing. Painless, objective. He looked so much older, more comfortable in his body, a shoe worn long enough, relaxed and suited to slightly larger, manly proportions. His chin stood out, defined, like a sculpture, his arms not too muscular but bulky, thick, healthy and the look on his face always adult and detached and disinterested.

He gave a cigarette to Walter on the bus like nothing, a piece of trash he was throwing away, another one already hanging from his mouth and seeming about to light itself, and then Tyler would be smoking right there, from his bus seat, and he wouldn't care and he wouldn't get caught. Because how could Tyler get in trouble for smoking a cigarette on the bus when Tyler's cigarette had just lit naturally, being exactly right, everything fitting the moment?

Walter caught the cigarette, badly, rolling the delicate piece of death in the inside of his hand, fighting his clumsiness not to crush it as he palmed it into his jean pocket. He attempted delicacy, trying too hard, failing while accomplishing what he had set out to do at the same time, pocketing the cigarette and enough tobacco poison collecting in the bottom of his jeans, the shreds maybe discovered later by Teresa, pulling his jeans from the dryer as the frayed brown-black tobacco bits spilled from the inside-out pockets, frowning, maybe, thinking, what was to be done with a boy that wasn't her responsibility?

On the porch of his father's house, dark, Walter smoked the single cigarette, savoring a prize he had fought hard for. Night, in the a.m. hours it burned, the orange flow flickered on and off to the tempo of his breath, the heartbeat of his lungs humming, he felt the flood of nicotine and whatever else overwhelm him, pounding at his senses. He was released again for only long enough.

He felt his face with his hands, discovering his features again, changed, slightly older than he remembered them from his last inspection. In the morning time mirror he studied the trembling, tired creases of skin that made up his expression, he knew he was well into it—teenage years. He knew everything was different now, whether he had wanted this or not. Soon more would be asked of him. And he felt like he had given life his everything so far but fallen flat on his face.

Everyone his enemy, everyone to be suspected, he watched his peers through the lens of paranoia. This lens lending lucidity to each situation. He understood now. He knew the rules because he made them up as he went and they completed him: if he scrubbed his hands viciously with soap in the gritty dirtiness of the school restroom; if he looked away when the girls caught him watching them; if he guessed at the unseen shape of them, imagining brushing up against the most beautiful ones (seemingly on accident) in the crowded hallways as all the students went to class; if he raised his hand and answered only the questions the teacher asked the classroom he was *certain* he knew, should know, nothing beyond the realm of knowledge of a fifteen-year-old boy; if he told his father nothing about his day at school when he was asked; if he escaped the ridicule of his peers through blending in, not in the sense of being one of them, but in the sense of being transparent, essentially not there; if he spoke to no one.

If.

Then he would be accepted. Then he would dissolve into the environment. No one could know anything about him ever, he had to hide the real him, a glimpse at it would give his intent away, would turn them all on him.

The girls noticed him, an accident, out the corner of an eye watching something else entirely, some dream that might have been remembered wrong.

There was a small girl, Allison, a mouse made unthreateningly human, small and brown and dull and speaking in a squeak, hidden behind glasses big enough to be a mask to her miniature face. He was waiting in the lunch line, waiting for an old skinny woman with her hair in a black mesh net to spoon macaroni on his plate. He could smell it hovering, orange and yellow, bright, flavorful in a horrible way.

"Walter," Allison squeaked at him, her voice like a highlighter squealing across the slick of a textbook page.

He did a double take, certain he had imagined that her voice had spoken his name, that she even knew his name, that even this pipsqueak of femininity had taken notice of his presence in the lunch line. Clearly, she was out of her place, standing aside from the line but facing him. Facing him and her body turned towards him and speaking his name. She spoke it again.

"Walter."

"Uh," he said, turning from the skinny old lunch lady serving him the glowing orange slop, "did you say my name?"

"Yes. Duh."

She paused to restart the conversation, implying his stupidity had impeded her from saying what she had to say. His cheeks beat at his face, heating themselves.

"Do you know Tori Ericson?"

"Tori Ericson. Tori Ericson." His head throbbed for an answer, his head continued to produce a question mark where should have been an exclamation point.

"She's in your gym class. She was a brunette but now she's blond. Real tall." The tiny girl looked him up and down. "Taller than you."

"Tori Ericson," he said, stupidly, trying to fight the blank image from his mind as if that would do anything, struggling with himself, deep and inward.

"She likes you."

The girl swirled around and walked away. A cloud of dust seemed to buoy up about him in her wake. Her words echoed, spoken as shrill as anything else little Allison said, almost unacceptable in their plainness, in how certain he was of exactly what they were and what they meant.

He carried them with him all the way to the cafeteria table where he sat, by himself, turning the words over and over in his mind, fighting to understand them more, to think what other meaning they could hold, weighing them, comparing them to other words that meant nothing to him now, judging them like that game the teachers in elementary school had played where he was asked to guess how many jelly beans were in the jar and then the jelly beans became his if he was correct or closest.

Was this a joke?

Could a girl like him?

Was that possible?

Tori. Tori Ericson. Of course he knew Tori Ericson. Her hair that unnatural, almost white blond not matching her face but making her skin stand out as if tan, but it wasn't: it was pale, pale, pale. No makeup. A yellow white, not papery, but yellow like light gold, like a glow that had turned into a color but still retained some whiteness. Her unusual skin carrying her like royalty, older than her somehow—a wedding dress she inherited.

Her body was tall, lean, meatless and light, about to drift away. But she was busty too, already with womanly breasts. Her legs were long and right and firm in her short gym shorts.

"How could *she* like *me*?" he said out loud. But somehow he didn't allow himself to doubt.

He went home and thought about her and imagined her body was his pillow, held it to him, squeezed the life from it. He thought of her. He turned her to legend in his mind, she grew more powerful, swallowing him, stealing sleep from him, becoming a presence over his shoulder, there with him, torturing him with ownership. He had handed her the keys to his soul because it was meaningless—the thing was worthless to him.

The next day she acknowledged him. He saw her continue to look his way as they sat cross-legged, far away, separated by students and sweat and body odor and the dusty slick of the gym floor stretching between them. She watched him. She seemed to speak to him a silent language she assumed he knew and he struggled to understand the far away movement of her, the twitching, the whispering to her little friend next to her, the smiling, gone in an instant. She flashed at him and then turned unreadable again, terrifying in the locked awayness of her.

What did it mean? Each moment was a test he was certain to fail.

A piece of a paper, a shredded piece of notebook paper, passed from student to student, all of them half asleep and probably none of them noticing even that their fingers passed across the note.

"This is for you," the boy sitting in front of him said in an indifferent baritone.

He opened the wrinkled bit of paper and read the words and

his breath slipped from him.

Did Allison tell you about how I like you?

The handwriting was a glorious curving, like a drawing made with a beautiful sense for shapes. The molding, the art in letters.

And looking up from the paper and catching his breath he saw she was watching him, smiling now, giving him all of her eyes.

She motioned to him, one elegant fist raised, one finger out pointing at him, pointing maybe at the paper.

Confused he tried to hand the paper back to the boy, the boy pushed it back on him, shaking his head.

"She wants you to write something back, man."

Walter nodded. Of course, that was how this worked. Of course, simple enough.

He looked around for a pen or a pencil, searching his empty gym short pockets. He frantically asked if anyone had something to write with. Someone passed a gnawed up pencil to him.

He wrote: *Yes, she did.*

He folded the paper back together and passed it down the line.

He watched her from across the gym room as her elegant fingers plucked apart the folded corners of the wrinkled notebook paper, delicate in their movement as if performing surgery, and he tried desperately to gauge the expression forming on her face as she read the three words he had written.

She seemed to do a thing with her mouth, an ambiguous thing, maybe a laugh. Was she laughing at him? He was empty, stupid, a hole to fall into with no bottom; he was dead to himself already after only fifteen years.

She wrote more and the paper made its way back through the passing of the hands.

Do you like me Walter?

He looked up at her and saw how closely she was watching him, how much she noticed him. It killed him to be noticed like this, the greatest pleasure he had known, he waited to wake up from this dream. Oh, to be noticed—to be seen against the grey of his life, to stand out in the middle of the blandness. He stood out to her and her emerald gaze; everything else disappeared.

He nodded his head to her emphatically.

She smiled at him across the room. Instantly the massive gymnasium seemed to empty except for the two of them.

Gym class began. The teacher had them walk or run a mile after stretching, but most of them walked, droning on, heads down, some beside each other talking, Walter usually alone, and alone now with the back of his head sprouting the lightest of wings that made him feel utterly away from himself and only watching, he walked and looked across the room at Tori, watching him behind the frame of her graceful, yellow skin.

She walked up to him and his life moved a split second faster than before.

The first time. She spoke to him.

"Walter. Meet me at lunch. You know where we sit."

She was gone without touching him. Though she hadn't really seemed about to, she could have been about to—this was a possibility. Maybe she would touch him at lunch. He imagined what her skin felt like.

"This is my new boyfriend," she introduced him to her friends. They were crows, dressed in black, rebels, dark and pale and skeptical.

But nice.

Allison was among them and gazed at him, smiling, with a knowing look in her eye like they had known each other a hundred years.

One of them studied him. "He looks like he'd be a good boyfriend. What's your name?"

"Walter," he said, meek as an apology.

"Huh," she said.

"He's cool," Allison said.

"What's your favorite color Walter?" another one crooned.

"Black," he said, without thinking, the exact right answer

slipping out of him, his unconsciousness plucking it from his mind. Absolutely *not* his favorite color, he realized.

"Ah."

"Oh."

"Yes!"

They all wilted at his answer, melting in their gothic chainmail: approval.

"He *is* cool," someone said.

He ate with them each day. A week passed.

One day at recess he walked beside her and she snatched his hand, violent almost, deliberate, demanding it into hers, clutching his, the animatronic grip swallowing his palm, her fingers twisting around his. The joined hands swung between them.

He felt electricity.

At home he dreamed of her, he imagined her body, he thought only of her, all other girls were not real, cut outs, paper dolls, flimsy, possessing no substance.

He could feel his desire for her at night in bed. This started as a tingling in his feet, so powerful he could trace the movement of it through his body. If there had been a diagram of his body in front of him, he could have drawn a line to represent the movement of this power.

The desire now traveled outside of him, causing the air around him to glow.

They had said almost no words to each other.

Finally she had his number. She asked him at lunch and he spat the digits out before she could finish asking. He waited for her call in the room in his father's house that had the phone, all the doors around him shut, an isolated room where he could hide and answer the phone before the first ring had finished.

"Hello?"

"Hey. Is this Walter?" Her voice, a swimming motion oozing with dignity through the holes in the phone and into his ear.

"Hey. Yes. I mean, yes. It's me."

"Oh. You sound different through the phone. Your voice, it's . . . deeper."

"Okay I didn't know that—"

"I wanted to talk to you. I wanted to talk to you so bad. I like how quiet you are, I love how quiet you are. But I thought it was sad how you would walk by yourself. I saw how you would walk by yourself, to gym, or after lunch, by yourself, and I wanted—"

"Oh. I was, I was just—"

"I saw how you would do that and I thought how interesting you looked, how sad you looked—"

"I wasn't really by myself, I was waiting for someone, I—"

"I saw that and I really wanted to find out more about you and I don't feel like I have at all. But your sadness, it is so—"

"I have friends, I was waiting on them to catch up with me. I got ahead of them."

"So *manly*." She sighed into the receiver of the phone and he listened unbelievingly.

"Tori."

"Yes, Walter?"

"I have friends. I wasn't by myself, really."

"Yes. Of course. Yes. I should tell you about *myself*." Her voice picked up and marched on. "I'm not like the other girls you know, the girls our age. I mostly like boys. I like boys for friends, isn't that weird? I don't like girls much, I eat with them at lunch, but mostly only the older ones, a couple years older at least, the ones that are different, not always talking about all that bullshit that girls talk about. I hate all that bullshit that girls talk about. I could give a fuck about the color pink, pillows, wearing makeup, boys liking me. I could give a fuck about *pink*! I don't want you to be afraid of me, but I want to tell you this. I want to tell you this, because you're interesting and I want you to know about me, more about me and what makes me *me*.

"I used to be a witch. I mean, a better way to say it is that I practiced witchcraft. Nothing too bad, I mean, I learned how to do some things from my sister, but I would never really do them. I just did harmless things. Like changing hair color for instance. Like making—"

"Wait, Tori?"

"Yeah, Hon?"

"What did you just say? Did you say you are a witch?" His brain struggled to work right, uncomprehending. It was failing him, clearly.

"Oh yes. I mean, no. I mean, I used to be Walter. I mean I learned a little bit about magic. But I didn't do anything bad, I would never do anything to you." She laughed, a drowning cackle, a well to fall into. "I mean. Let's see. Let's talk about something else."

Her voice plodded on into the night, an hour went by. Two.

She told him about drinking a handful of times, that she had never smoked pot even though her older friends all did, an older boy who slept on her couch when her father was gone but the boy had thought that she had been about to let him sleep in her bed with her, the trailer park where she lived, boyfriends throughout middle school, a black boyfriend that her father almost beat up when he came over, her father's ignorant glare jailing her to her room. Walter couldn't call her either, she explained, her father would know.

"I mean, sometimes, sure, you can call. I mean, just only at the right time. When he isn't here. We'll talk about it more, we'll figure it out."

He hung up the phone finally, glad his father hadn't walked in on the awkwardly insane attentiveness with which he had held the phone to his ear, and he sighed and thought about her and knew she was totally crazy and he was crazy for her.

He fell into the future of his life.

Her hand grasped his the next day, alien, new, cold to the touch, freezing him, the cold moving up through him.

She was taking him over and he didn't care.

And in the same breath, she grew boring.

As everything was lost in the conquering, the light not there when you closed your fingers around it and then reopened them to an empty palm. The firefly died in the little jar. His iridescent magnificence extinguished in captivity.

What was he supposed to do?

Kiss her?

The most dangerous thing he could imagine. And impossible for a slew of reasons: 1) he would be bad at it; 2) he had never tried to before; 3) the instant he tried, she would laugh at him; 4) he still faintly suspected that possibly she didn't like him at all, and this whole thing had been a set up from the moment when he tried to kiss her to when she would laugh at him and spit in his face; 5) this idea violated every natural instinct he possessed, to dare to do something so *new*.

They walked hand in hand from the lunchroom, day in day out, silent, silence stretching out over the fear in his life as if that fear could protect him when he knew it could not and had no power; he wielded no power at all, though silence came closest to being of any use to him. The only excitement he knew the touch of her hand, the cool of her palm on the way to recess after lunch.

She hugged him once, hard, taller and spilling over him, clutching him.

Little Allison came to him the next day.

"Tori's breaking up with you," she said. She scurried off.

He did not cry. It would be stupid to cry. This was a nothing, a flake on his life, a stray piece of lint picked from his clothes, an emptiness inflicted on an emptiness. To cry would be like erasing the blankness off a fresh piece of paper.

He watched Tyler enviously in math class. The robot of him, the power of his not caring, the sweet indifference defying existence to blemish it.

Tyler finally noticed Walter's blank stare.

"What are you looking at, kid?"

Walter chewed at his lip, fearing the next question but

powerless to stop that it was about to be asked. "Whatever happened to Smiley?"

Tyler's eyes clouded over, the indifference in them perhaps flickering off for a second. "He doesn't go to school."

"Where is he?" Walter asked.

The moisture in them grew, but it seemed like Tyler's eyes themselves got larger, bulging out of his head in their shape.

"I don't know where he is," Tyler said. "I ain't got a fuckin' clue, kid."

"Watch your mouth Tyler," the teacher snapped. Both their heads turned up, unaware that any of the words had been caught by a third party. "That means detention again."

CHAPTER IV
Body of the Swan

Time passed. It had to, running in a current, not stopping for Walter to catch his breath. Time regarded him as would an ancient giant noticing a dandelion he did not particularly want to step on, pausing in the journey north just long enough to watch the placement of his massive toes on the earth.

Walter allowed that hiccup of a moment, that pause, only here could his breath come. Forced to learn to breathe underwater to save himself from drowning. He found that the days did not end, instead growing longer. His shadow stretching out from under him, a man chained to him trying to grow out of the shackles, not really mimicking his movement but clownishly reacting to it, not copying—but interpreting. His shadow grew long with the cold moving back into the ground, the poison of its affair spreading and turning hard as rock. The world was flat, the world was ugly, so winter reminded him. He seemed the only living thing here, wandering about in search of another survivor.

The year 2001 had come.

Walter must learn to drive a car now—so his father explained, calmly, carefully, like a man evacuating a building about to explode, trying to speak sense into the mob of a crowd—he could already have had his permit, had he put forth the effort a year ago.

They arranged themselves inside his father's car, gingerly, approaching the metal, man-made hunk like the enemy, careful not to incite anger. Walter felt bizarre, like something horrifically wrong being in the driver's seat. The car reacted to the touch of the brake, to the touch of the gas like a consciousness that Walter was communicating with. The car jutted and bumped, breathing clumsily. The groan of the engine was certainly a language. The car existed next to him, around him, he learned to caress it. Driving a car was not like working a regular machine, not like pressing a series of buttons. Driving was a cool and slow dance, the wearing of a man's body your entire life then suddenly having to cast it aside and slip into a woman's fragile, delicate body with a mind of its own, jerking away from his ogre touch, stuttering under the tap of the brakes, convulsing as he pressed the gas pedal too hard, gliding, a huge clumsy swan on the road under his misguided touch.

Two cars on the other side of the road coming toward him, not there a moment before. This was a dagger half an inch away from his eyeball, he swerved over the grass of the yard to the left of them. There was a mailbox. He swerved off the yard again, foot to gas, still going. He didn't look back to try and find the mailbox, in the street or in the yard. Had there been a mailbox at all? He wasn't sure.

His father shouted at him to stop.

He slammed on the brakes and both of their heads bobbed.

In the middle of the barren neighborhood road, his father ripped open the door and walked around the car and banged on the driver's side window. The moment Walter had the door slightly ajar he felt himself yanked from the seat. He was being shaken hard. His father's words seemed more violent than the shaking though, and they beat about his brain as if trying to infiltrate his fragilely guarded psyche. He could not repeat a word of the painful frenzy but he knew that his father had never spoken to him like this before. The possibility of actual violence burned through his words, heat beneath them, cooking them to a crisp, blackened nonsense. Meaning seemed gone from them.

He felt the marks of his father's fingers continue to ache when he was released. He stumbled into a pile of body parts on the street underneath them. His father had chewed on him for a moment and spat him out.

He did not wait for Walter to get back up before putting himself in the driver's seat.

Walter uncrumbled himself and doggedly went to his rightful place, the passenger's seat.

His father's face red as the devil's all four minutes of the ride back.

Walter raised a hand to feel the bruise where his father's touch sizzled over his skin, but then he felt shame at his pitifulness and lowered his hand and let the pain sink into him, knowing it was exactly what he deserved. He wished he were someone else. Mostly he was shamed for his father, who had to live with having been a part of the collaboration that had brought him into existence.

■ ■ ■

A driving class began. A private class, not at the high school. At dinner time, six o'clock. A family run business, wife and husband, both pushing three hundred pounds and under six feet tall. Mr. and Mrs. Lancaster's school of driving.

The class was shown a video of a woman being hit by a train.

In a rush the woman darts across the tracks while a crowd waits on the other side. There is not time for anyone to shout. Her body transforms into a brown cloud. The cloud of brown does not remotely resemble a human being.

The VHS tape was undeniably real in the grainy resolution, authentic, shown to the class as a scare tactic of some kind. Children, look both ways.

Walter marveled at the tape and that he was not bothered at all by watching a human being explode right in front of him. There was something fascinating about how detached he was from watching and knowing this was truly the end of a human's life, he witnessing their final moment.

Mrs. Lancaster left the room after showing the tape, frowning with seriousness, answering a phone ringing in the other room. One of the students, skinny and goofy, the class clown, stood from his desk. He stumbled to the VCR and rewound the tape and—with a horrific smile of delight—the class collectively witnessed the brown cloud, once more. The footage barely lasted a second, seeming shorter this time, over before it began, deceptive.

The boy rewound the tape again, paused it and excitedly put his finger on the screen, speaking in a loud whisper, his finger on the blurred smudge of washed out color, "That's a piece of her brain."

⁘ ⁘ ⁘

Walter found himself in the car—wielding a student driver triangle on top—with Mr. Lancaster. He felt more in control of the vehicle than ever before, as if he had only to think to move the car forward. This was not necessarily a good thing; the power was overwhelming and terrifying. He felt unready for it.

He slammed on the brakes hard enough to make both of their heads yank from their necks for an uneasy second. He slammed on the brakes when *he* was the one with the right of way and there was no stop sign as the neighborhood road formed a cross with the next neighborhood road, the old woman frowning at him through her car window, waiting for him to go, sitting at her stop sign.

Thinking of the mailbox that may or may not have existed, he hit the gas first like the head of a child he was tapping awake lightly with his foot. Then he gave in. He pressed down. He felt his foot changing, transforming underneath the weight of his long life. He felt his foot fusing with the gas pedal, making it a part of him. He was the car.

He heard his father's voice alongside him, battering him with vicious words that he swatted away using the speed he had become one with.

"What are you doing son?"

His head jolted back, removed from the joints and the sockets and then stuffed back into them, the wires that made up his body yanked and then fused back.

"Slow down, *boy*."

Walter looked over at Mr. Lancaster. The fat of the man spilled through the frame of his body, his skin a pure, white sickliness.

"What the hell is wrong with you?" The voice in his head and outside of his head. His head had become a heartbeat.

"You don't go that fast. Ever."

When Mr. Lancaster spoke, the fat of his chin moved as if he were a massive puppet being operated by a man behind him. Walter studied him. There was something animatronic about him, the art of someone else seemed written in his features. Jim Henson maybe.

"Don't look at me fucktard, look at the road."

The car grew hot with his fat hate turning alive, growing physical tentacles that reached out and tickled Walter's cheek.

Walter's eyes shut with the resolve of hands closing over a throat.

He felt his body jerk from the seat, held back only by the belt. He felt the sound of the tires screeching before he heard them. It ripped through him, a sound that split him in half, dividing him for the sake of creating a new him. He could not resume existing until it was over, through him, trapped in the sound for the several seconds of its roar. He would never be the same, of course.

"You failed."

His eyes still closed.

■ ■ ■

It did not come as a surprise: by now he had discovered that he failed at everything he tried at least once.

After suffering through three more weeks and a number of four letter words from Lancaster, the road safety test stared up at Walter from his desk. Pencils scrawling throughout the faux classroom, the teens buried in this rite of passage, the test that would legally unleash them into the vehicular realm of adulthood.

The Scantron sheet lay before Walter with its intense, papery smell waiting to be saturated in the lead of the number two pencil he clutched too tightly, to the point that his fingers began to smart. On the sheet at the top was each letter in the alphabet, contained in a bubble, with instructions to fill in the bubbles that corresponded with his full name.

Around him he heard the soft but busy scraping of his peer's pencils, digging into the test questions. He felt that he was already losing to them as he filled in the letter bubbles that matched up with his name. His mind whirled.

When may you drive off the road to pass another vehicle?

But when would he dare to pass any vehicle ever, when would he presume he deserved a spot in front of another, potentially more competent driver, occupying space on the road already in front of him?

A) If the shoulder is wide enough to accommodate your vehicle. B) If the vehicle ahead of you is turning left. C) Under no circumstances.

Certainly C, the only possible answer! He filled in the bubble for C.

After that, questions came out of the blue, mercilessly materializing before him, darting in and out of his mind without a warning—

What should you do when you are driving at night? A) Make sure you are driving slow enough so you can stop within the range of your headlights. B) Roll down your window so that the air will keep you awake. C) Drink coffee.

When you are merging onto the freeway, you should be driving: A) At or near the same speed as traffic on the highway. B) 5 to 10 miles slower than traffic on the highway. C) The posted speed limit for traffic on the highway.

When driving in a fog, what should you use? A) Fog lights. B) High beams. C) Low beams.

He scratched his head at them. He went to look for the knowledge or experience or plain common sense in him, anything in him buried down there, anything useful that he could dredge up, that he could use to fill in an answer bubble with confidence, with assurance that he knew anything at all, that a shred of him had learned something, having taken away a piece of knowledge from the previous classes, the exploding train woman, the frown on Mr. Lancaster's face as he proceeded to lecture and curse and have his fat face flush red at Walter.

There seemed to be nothing inside of him, nothing at all.

In the end, he just picked C for most answers. He ended up passing the test by one question. His failure at having learned anything was minimal enough to allow him to move on to the next step—

The actual driver's license test.

The first time alongside the halfway pretty woman from the DMV, fortyish, her silvery yellow hair pulled back in single, economic ponytail, he botched up the three-point turn miserably. During this moment in the test, she stoically observed his confusion, the look on his face of chaotic thinking, forehead crinkled like he had never heard of the maneuver before. He made the act into more of a five-point turn. Braking and turning again and backing up again and frowning and crinkling his forehead further, deeper, his look growing more serious. She continuing to observe.

The look of her patient indifference was more painful than Lancaster's exasperation with his idiocy.

"You failed," she said flatly. "Mainly because of the three-point turn."

He came back the next day.

The second time he passed, pulling off the three-point turn flawlessly (he had practiced in the mean time with his father barking all the way out the driveway).

Thank God North Carolina does not require parallel parking— his final thought on the matter.

■ ■ ■

All this so Walter could drive himself to school with a smile on his face, eyes peeled open in a desperate exertion of will power over his inability to be a member of society, to operate as everyone else did.

He *must* pay attention. He *must* pay attention to everything—such was the rule of survival.

He learned the code of road life; this was the same code to all life as far as he knew—fear.

He drove Teresa's car to school—she with no need for the thing being currently jobless and drooped over his father's couch like a pile of clothes his father didn't remember owning.

The car had fast food hamburger wrappers in unknown corners of the interior, hiding carefully, perched and waiting for his hand to slip into the crack searching for the button to release the trunk or the gas valve. An aged fry turned to rock. Or he accidently stumbled on little slivers here and there of the feminine world so alien to Walter—a tampon, a pink sock the size of a baby fist, a hair pin.

On his way back from school in her car one afternoon, he gazed out the window at a stoplight, his sight drawn to the morning sun on his eyelashes, blinking, framing his vision, the car next to him coming into focus.

A Nissan. Black and dusty yellow with spring's vomited pollination. The rearview mirror vibrated in a motion that seemed violent somehow to Walter. Rap music, barely discernible through the massive level of volume it had reached, shook the air around the two cars sitting at the stoplight.

Walter wiggled his nose at the cigarette smoke that trickled over him.

The car was occupied by Tyler. Still no Smiley, only Tyler by himself, smoking his cigarette, that lack of emotion to his features, chiseled from stone. As always he stared through the horizon line.

Walter studied him, fascinated though he could not understand or explain his obsession with the older boy. He hadn't seen him since Tyler had dropped out of high school.

He did not notice Walter.

The light turned green and his car rolled on, music trailing down the road.

Walter tapped his knee, no rhythm to his beat, perhaps impatient that he was here with his father, perhaps impatient that he was still alive. He had been alive for fifteen years—dangerously close to sixteen now—and believed that everything that could happen to a living creature had happened to him. Other than sexual intercourse.

He waited in the church hallway. His ass sore with the shape of the bench etching itself into him. His father was inside the room next door, speaking with the pastor of the church.

Outside, August had begun to conquer the summer with the weapon of wind, leaving a trail of blood-colored leaves.

He wished it were winter.

Winter was the only time he was permitted to be himself, the true him tucked underneath reality, no danger of being discovered.

Instead, fall forced him to conform to the hustle of real life, the clicking of school pens, the ruffle of papers tattooed in lead, whispers of his peers.

His inability to conform to these things was really the reason he found himself in this odd excuse for a church, even odder excuse for a school. He would probably be attending here from now on. The place was warehouse-like and bare, located on the other side of town from where they lived. Recommended to his father by a friend of Teresa's at the moment when the computer of Walter's mind became no longer able to process the public school system. He stopped going. Or more like he became unable to move from bed the day that a bully pulled down his shorts in gym and everyone saw his penis.

Walter did not try to listen to the conversation taking place between his father and the pastor in the room, and—once he became aware that the mumbling sound was their conversation—

he shut his eyes, tight. He closed them with the powerful energy of turning away, imagining he could relinquish control over the opening of them simply in the surrender to that power. But when he heard the door creak open, his eyelids snapped loose and his vision was flooded.

His father stood in the doorway.

"It's settled," he said. "You start Monday."

Walter looked to his feet for comfort and saw nothing but the dirty white of his tennis shoes looking back up at him, one of them with the laces untied. He leaned into it, about to retie it. Then he thought better of this and straightened his back and rose from the bench.

The day was Sunday, nearly an hour after a strange service had taken place.

Walter and his father had caught the tail end of it, a bearded man dancing in the aisle. Amen, amen and words of nonsense (tongues?) and other things reverberated through the hallway, things Walter had assumed religious people were only rumored to do. How could human beings be such animals and believe themselves anything different, that anything they said had been pulled from anywhere other than the parts of their brain they weren't even supposed to use?

In the car on the way home, Walter broke the hideous silence, thick and fuzzy and mind-numbing, between him and his father.

"But we don't even go to church."

His father sighed and waited for the silence to settle, to grow over the words, to blur them. Then he interrupted the quiet, cutting its life short. But the spoken words were merely accentuating the void of communication between father and son.

"Try to learn something from this place."

Silence soaked his words like a sponge.

"I'm doing this for you," he added, awkwardly, as the car hummed along, plodding their way home. The end to something hovered over them.

"I'm doing this for you, goddammit!" he said again.

His father was angry at the something that hovered over him. Maybe the echoing quiet, that dangerous creature they had birthed.

No, that had been there millions of years before, slinking its way out of the slime, existing before sound, an invisible thing more essential than air, around since the beginning.

Perhaps *that* was this God everyone spoke so much about, thought Walter.

Silence.

His own personal interpretation, his religion.

When they were home at last, his father handed him over to Teresa like a sack of food he had carried a long way on his back, something important but exhausting, something he was eager to be rid of.

There was a dress code and they had to shop for the right sort of clothes, clothes he would blend in with, clothes considered *acceptable*. The goal was to go unnoticed, to become one of them, or at least give off the outward impression that he was a part of the crowd.

In Teresa's dusty yellow car, the color of pollen, she chattered away eagerly, squirrel-like in her nervous youthfulness, she spat forth questions like a machine that couldn't be turned off once started.

"What do you think of this church you are going to go to school at? Great Blessings or Great Tidings or somethin'?"

Walter: "Fine."

"Wasn't Pastor George nice to you?"

"I didn't talk to him."

"So you start tomorrow?"

"Yep."

"Well are you glad they accepted you?"

Walter allowed a pause where he looked from the car window to Teresa's young face; she seemed twice as young as him.

"Ecstatic." His voice dripped.

She looked away from him, eyes on the road, all the cars conjoining as if becoming a universal consciousness for half a second, as if everyone in a car in Wilmington were suddenly aware of Walter's plight. She ignored his ugly sarcasm as long as she could.

Then she could not any longer, smacking the dashboard with her palm, the skin of her face flushing fiery red.

"You little shit!"

Walter allowed his frown to turn into a soft smile. He resisted the urge to laugh.

Later, in JCPenney, he refused to be the one to pick out the clothes. Noiselessly, she did the work for him, uncomplaining of his nonparticipation, barely observing him while she flipped through the racks of collared shirts and khakis, setting aside a pair here and there. Her brief outburst from before had been discarded from her mood. He hung alongside her, quiet but present.

She touched his arm to draw him to her for a moment of wonderful awkwardness. Like static electricity, he felt more than the physicality of her touch reaching into him. Who she was, this was him too. Where did the moment come from, what caused it to be different from any other moment between them? In an instant he understood: she wanted to be okay with him. She wanted them to coexist, and for her life was *also* difficult. In a different way, but difficult. Somehow through that touch he felt all these things passing into him.

Her other outstretched arm held several neatly folded, formal-looking clothes. Shirts with collars and khakis of the most dull, neutral colors imaginable—greyish brown, brownish grey, brownish brown.

She looked at him gently, all pretense suddenly dropping from the way she watched him. For this, he was grateful.

"You want to try these on in the dressing room? I think they are what you'll need."

"Not really," he told her. He had no need to be dishonest with her after the moment they had shared, and she knew this.

"Take them anyways." She clicked her tongue between sentences, dumping the clothes over one of his shoulders because he would not extend his hands to catch them. "Try them on. Should be the right size but won't know for sure until you put them on."

He looked a little confused, different from the usual robotic face he reserved for time spent with her. As if a wall had been penetrated though not broken down.

The dressing room minutes later. He watched the horrifically formal clothes sagging over his small body in the mirror. Teresa had picked the sizes by assuming the clothes should be a few sizes smaller than his usual wear; this meant, of course, they were still much too large for him.

He frowned at the image of himself reflected in the mirror, disappointed at the sight of himself, though he wasn't sure why.

He unzipped the black khakis he had on and they slid down his legs to his ankles.

"Are you almost done in there?" came Teresa's voice from the hallway.

He did not answer, but slid his feet from the bunched up khakis and felt them tumble underneath him.

"Does everything fit okay?"

He closed his eyes, not wanting to see himself in the mirror anymore. He waited for her to talk again, anticipating the moment. Something in her voice comforted him, even though he still didn't feel like responding to her.

"Are you okay?" Her voice was very close this time and he opened his eyes, even though he still didn't feel like responding to her.

"Walter?!"

He had left his eyes closed longer than he thought, and now she had entered the dressing room.

She was standing over him. He remembered how young she was again, and that he was attracted to her. She was tall and twenty-nine, her stockinged thighs eye-level with him.

Without wanting to, he imagined her panties underneath. What color they were. If she looked down she would probably notice the tent he was pitching, wearing nothing but a collared shirt and boxers.

He reached a hand out to feel the fabric of her stockings, lust flickering across his eyes, the shape of her legs—a dark tan, satiny mountain.

She smacked his wrist and looked angrily at him. He put his head down and she could see he was, of course, still hard.

The anger passed.

"I'm sorry," she said softly. "I shouldn't touch you like that. It's just—you looked like you were about to—"

He looked back up at her, a little hopeful despite himself at the change in her tone.

"I—" she started and stopped, realizing it in a slow beat. She had a hand on his shoulder, but this did nothing to help the situation if she was trying to avert what seemed teetering on the brink of happening. "Walter. . ." She squeezed his shoulder. "Have you felt like this since the beginning?"

He nodded his head, a child caught in the act of sneaking candy underneath his pillow.

He expected her to scold him at this revelation. Instead her hand moved across him, the finger on it daintily trickling down him, tracing his youthfully sized shape, moving down him, down. Maybe he imagined it—because he was looking up and not down— but he thought he felt the flicker of her finger across that hard key to his soul.

He did. Didn't he? He sensed her gripping him, squeezing for a millisecond that he would never know for a genuine sensation or an imagined one.

She leaned in as if about to kiss him and he let out a low, low groan. She retracted. Had she been about to kiss him? At the same time the question came to him, he felt himself emptying, that private thing happening to him. He forced himself to cough, as if that could prolong the little explosion. But it had already occurred.

He blushed and looked down.

From the look on her face, she knew what had happened. He was a little mad at her, had she orchestrated the humiliating experience on purpose, to gain power over him, to shame him in front of her?

"Oh Walter," she touched his fiery cheek, caressing it. "I'll get you some fresh underwear. You can wear it out. Wait here a second."

She whirled around, the dressing room door swinging shut behind her, leaving him there with himself. His stupid self.

He made a promise to himself:

If his father ever saw him in a moment like this one, he would kill himself.

In his new collared shirt, Walter attended schoolchurch the next day with a skeptical hum to his being, a light fluttering on and off but refusing to die, the repetitive slow torture that life was.

He would melt into the routine here as he would anywhere, any school. He would become the school, though it was different from what he was used to in the past. Same difference. Different sameness.

The place looked empty with people in it, not like a school and certainly not like a church. Like a warehouse with desks and chairs arranged. About twenty young people, from adolescence to teenagers, huddled around the desks. A single whiteboard was at the front.

At each desk—a stack of color-coded workbooks. One spine green, one red, one blue.

The teacher had not arrived yet, or maybe there wouldn't be a teacher.

That first day at school he noticed a skinny thing, cheeks pockmarked, some sort of excuse for girl, the hint of familiarity in her face, in her eyes. About his age, sitting at the desk. Scratching her mouse brown hair.

He was entirely unattracted to her.

But something drew him to her mediocre vibe, her plainness, so he sat down right next to her.

"Walter!" she squealed.

"Huh?" He looked at her.

"It's me, Alice." She frowned. "Remember me?"

Alice, Ugly Alice. He found the parts of her that he recognized and tried to put them together, constructing the old her for the sake of his memory. The pieces did not seem to match and he had to sort of force them, like taking a puzzle piece and wedging it into the wrong spot.

"Oh," he said.

His mind swirled in the horror of the past, memory churning inside him, the re-experience new again, graciously unremembered.

"Do you remember me?"

He narrowed his eyes at her as if to signal he did not. Or—as was actually true—that he would *rather* not.

"Yeah," he said. "Sort of."

"Well, I remember you," she said.

"You were the one they called Ugly Alice?"

She nodded, slowly watching him, somehow without a frown.

"You used to be fat," he said, not meaning to be untactful, but once his words had come out that way he was kind of glad. Perhaps his rudeness would deter her from further contact.

She was unruffled. "Go fuck yourself." But she said this cheerily. He felt as though he was instantly her friend again, roped in, trapped, restrained.

He stood up and went to another desk.

■ ■ ■

The schoolchurch becoming routine, becoming his life, inside of him laying eggs that would hatch snakes coiling through his intestines, poisonous fangs sinking into his heart. Poison that did not kill or cripple. Poison that converted. The only kind of poison that mattered . . .

He stayed away from Alice. He could almost see tears in her eyes from across the room. He knew what had happened to her. Her story achieved a legendary status among their peers. She had tried to off herself, quite unsuccessfully, swallowing a bottle or so of aspirin. They pumped her stomach at the hospital and she went from that hospital to the kind of one where there was nothing physically wrong with the patients, the Loony Bin as his mother called it (who knew exactly what to call the place with the drooling, medicated patients because she had been there herself more than once).

He tried not to think about his mother; he had not heard from her in a long time. He tried not to imagine what debauchery she may have fallen into by this time.

How Alice ended up in this schoolchurch, a drop in the ocean, a city away, it was almost too horrible.

They tore their way through the workbooks, answering questions that always cycled back to Christianity somehow, even the math ones. Everything looking for an excuse to slither the word God into the equation, to remind the student of the greater purpose that threaded life together. The workbooks—annoyingly—overutilized exclamation points.

Math:

Men, using the abilities God gave them, have developed methods for solving multiplication problems. But if we have only learned to manipulate numbers on a piece of paper, we have missed out. We have missed learning to use multiplication in the tasks God has given us to do!

A multiplication method will only work if it accurately describes the way God causes objects to multiply. If God were not faithfully holding all things together, reducing multiplication to a method would be impossible!

How is it that so many different people have found all these mathematical methods to reach the same answer? Each of these methods ultimately works because *it rests on God's faithfulness in holding all things together!*

Language Arts:

God gave us language so that we might communicate with one another! God gave us many forms of language to match the complexity of our thoughts.

Break down the grammar of this paragraph. Identify the nouns, verbs and explain how the placement of these allows it to be easily read and understood:

In the beginning was the Word, and the Word was with God, and the Word was God. The same was in the beginning with God. All things were made by him; and without him was not any thing made that was made. In him was life; and the life was the light of men. And the light shineth in darkness; and the darkness comprehended it not.

Not retching over the pages was—for him—a constant struggle. Or to rip them out of their brightly colored spine. To shred them in his hands and cackle at his power to destroy them so easily.

Not that he had anything against religion or Christianity.

Or even a concept of God. Walter could get down with the possibility of a God, this thought seemed not unreasonable. Sure, he had contemplated the possibility of there *not* being one too. But whatever there was, there had to be something somewhere more than humans, who were weak and flawed and cruel to each other. If that was the greatest thing the universe held, you could go ahead and count Walter out as being a participant.

All that had nothing to do with his irritation.

The irritation came at being forced to write out an answer to these thinly veiled questions, with their biblical allusions and their way of steering his answer. Each one made him a little more dishonest with himself every time. Not totally brainwashing him, no. But the questions were like a forceful creepy old man who followed him everywhere, looking over his shoulder at everything he did, assuming he completely understood the boy and already knew what Walter's reaction would be to anything that could happen to him. And he was always uncomfortably nudging him and grinning at him and assuming they were both in perfect agreement about all things.

Adults stepped in and out of the "classroom," occasionally asking a question to a student, almost never addressing all twenty of them at once, but just passing through.

Mostly they made their way through the stack of workbooks utterly unsupervised, and in silence, not communicating with each other or making eye contact. The room had an air of imprisonment, though no one was sure what kept them there, as though all the students were in an unlocked cell—the cage door swinging open— and they knew there was a consequence for leaving but they didn't know what, the uncertainty keeping them in place. There was a table right by the one bathroom in the building. On that table were all the answer books to every single workbook that existed, a workbook for every grade from elementary school to the last year of high school.

The answer books were also organized by their colors, easy to find—Walter simply matched up the purple shade of the book he just finished with its twin.

At the end of each day he had to match up his answers with the ones in the answer books. On the table was a pencil holder full of red pens. This was how the adults were supposed to prevent the students from cheating; any corrections made after cross-referencing with the answer books were to be made in red ink. And the answers the students came up with themselves could only be written in pencil. With no pencils allowed at the answer table, this made it difficult to cheat.

After a while, Walter obtained a flawless system of going up to the answer table and copying the answers into his workbook with a mechanical pencil that had a red stem. He was never noticed, though not much attention was paid to him in the first place, at least not by anyone other than Ugly Alice.

September, another month that meant nothing to him, began and passed with that horrific, irreparable movement that belonged to time. Time could not be rewound, and as the present continued to happen to him, the past barely existed. Perhaps there was nothing behind him. Perhaps the things that happened, these things he clung so hard to as though they were all he had, were not there at all, an imagined stalker colored by paranoia. Nothing behind when he looked. To look comforted him no longer than a second and he still felt the eyes at his back when he turned around.

One morning, after driving Teresa's car to schoolchurch, he walked into a room full of faceless students. Each child had his or her head pressed flat to their desk. There was one single adult standing at the front of the room by the whiteboard—the pastor. His eyes were closed and his head was bowed so deeply it lolled from his body, about to roll right off his neck.

"What's going on?" stammered Walter, looking around. He set his book bag at an unoccupied desk.

"Quiet children!" snapped the pastor. His eyes did not open though his head lifted long enough for him to push the two words out in a shrill bark.

Walter looked around, trying to find the only student he knew by name, Ugly Alice. She was difficult to identify with only the top of her head visible, but he knew her tangled, boringly brown head of hair well enough that he recognized it. He crept over to her, leaving his book bag behind.

He tapped her shoulder gently.

Not a hint of movement betrayed her stasis.

He leaned to her ear and whispered, "Alice. It's me, Walter."

She moved her head slightly, her eyes rolling open and peeking up at him from the side, covert, the obvious fear of discovery in them.

"We're praying," she whispered. "Go to your desk and put your head down."

"I don't understand," he whispered back. "This is not how we usually do it."

"Something terrible has happened. A bunch of people just died," she said, her voice peppered with dread older than both their years combined. "We are praying for retribution."

He looked at her, baffled. "I don't understand. What happened?"

"Go to your desk and put your head down," she hissed. "Now. You'll get us both in trouble."

He kept looking at her, expecting maybe a little more of an explanation. But her eyes flipped back down and she was quiet. The room was quiet.

He stood in the quiet a few more seconds, waiting for someone to explain.

Then he crept back to the desk where his book bag was, tip-toeing, careful to barely move as was essential to reach the desk and sit. He looked around one time before putting his head down with everyone else.

The dark of having his head down—even when he blinked his eyes shut for as long as he could stand—was not a complete dark, was not a dark that shut out that horrible, confusing world around him. He longed for a complete dark. This *praying* notion he interpreted as a poor excuse for a more complete escape, escape into another world he had found only a time or two in his short life— namely, the times he had experienced drugs or alcohol.

He had surgery at age eleven—a quick, elegant operation to remove a benign tumor on his back. This had been the most complete and beautiful dark he ever knew, he went into it, triumphant, happily, a smile on his face as his vision of the nurse's face grew blotchy and tinted a dull orange. Everything went out in the time after that. The world was gone, gone and removed. He floated, even less than floated. He was not there.

He longed for this sort of dark now, his head over his crossed arms, waiting for anything to explain what was going on.

Finally, after what seemed to be hours and hours, he heard the pastor's voice rising above the hollow hush of the child infested room.

"Lord be with us on this dark day. This dark, dark, dark day. As dark as many of the days to come before Your son returns to us.

"Be with us and be with our families. Families who—on this day—lost their children, their mothers, their fathers, their brothers, their sisters. Be with them. Let them feel the love and reassurance of You, let them breathe easy knowing that Your vengeance will come on Your enemies!

"It will be swift when it comes! It will be great; it will sweep over the nation of our enemies and decimate them. We are surely close to the end times, and Your enemies cannot survive them.

"In Jesus' name we pray, Amen."

Walter was even more confused, but he lifted his head with everyone else.

The pastor looked out on the scared crowd of children. "Any questions before we get started?"

One little boy, probably aged about seven, raised his hand.

"Yes Sam."

The boy spoke in a barely audible squeal, like a puppy achieving human speech. "Should we pray for the people in the plane who died?"

"We just did Sam." Walter could feel the pastor rolling his eyes at the boy, even though he didn't visibly.

"I mean the other people on the plane. . ." the boy trailed off. His lip quivered, afraid to ask the question but clearly wanting to. "They died on the plane too. What about their families?"

"The terrorists?! Pray for the terrorists!"

"Aren't we supposed to forgive everybody?"

"Um, they will get what they have coming to them, son. They will get what they have coming to them."

"What is that? What do they have coming?"

His face went red, the color of blood, not the inhabitation of blood, but like his skin became a bloody mass. "Fire! Fire and brimstone await them. They went to their deaths expecting to wake up peacefully in a bed of roses, to forty virgins. There is a surprise or two God has in the wing for them. Do you understand boy?"

Sam looked terrified, gulping.

"No," he said.

"You'd better understand! You'd better! That is my job here, to *make* you understand. These are matters of grave importance. Look at this."

The pastor turned on a small television beside him.

Two extremely tall buildings appeared on the screen, exploding, shrinking underneath the cloud, like the bottoms had been cleanly removed and the top halves of the buildings just dropped.

"You see this! You see this! We are in the end times. That is how serious this is. This concerns all of us."

He left the TV on, playing in the background while his speech consumed its own words, becoming something separate from him, something hideously sentient with its own breath.

Walter stopped paying attention and looked behind him at the images on the screen. He saw the vast clouds of a leftover explosion settling across what was left of the buildings and spreading through this city he had never been to and had no connection to. He knew something terrible had happened, something beyond him, much larger than him, looming over his small life and not even noticing it.

He tried to feel sad.

He tried to make himself cry, seeing other students around him were. He tried to think the situation into a reality for him, not a thing far off that seemed like it hadn't happened at all, like a lie made up by adults, another one of their many tricks of the hand in the game they played, the pretend line of communication that didn't really exist between him and them. He tried so hard to care.

But he couldn't.

Not unlike the video he had seen of the woman who had exploded when she was hit by a train, it was not something that mattered to him—even though everything around him screamed that it should matter.

■ ■ ■

Instead of requiring completion of any work that day, the pastor announced that schoolchurch was over for the rest of the afternoon once he finished his rant. Walter went cautiously back to Alice's desk.

"Yes?" Alice said. She looked surprised.

"Remember when I went to your house?"

"Um. Yes." She looked down.

"Remember when we smoked that stuff?" His brain flickered, wanting the nothingness again, the lovely nothingness.

"Yes." She was starting to blush under the scars of her pimples.

"I want to do that again," he said excitedly. "Do you still have something like that?"

She shook her head.

"Oh." He looked very disappointed, his face hanging low.

She looked at him, sympathetic. "I have pills now. Sometimes I do those. I get them from my grandmother. I can bring you some tomorrow."

"What kind of pills?" he asked.

"They are called Oxycodone."

"I want them," he said, almost interrupting her.

■ ■ ■

When she finally remembered to bring him a handful of the little things, he kept them in his pocket for a week, achieving the balancing act of living life like he did not possess something so forbidden. He knew his father would be furious with these actions.

Then after school, one lonesome night.

In relief he clutched a single pill to his sweaty palm, a little powder bleeding off on his skin, hiding himself in his own room, locking the door, as if his father were home, which he wasn't.

He opened his hand and looked at the little yellow circle of salvation.

Opened his mouth and pressed his hand to it.

No water.

It tasted horrible.

He waited for the dark to come to him, the only is there was.

CHAPTER VI

Graduation and Gratitude

Moving into his future became more like time traveling than simply living—still being alive the next day then the next one. The dystopia Walter had only read about in science fiction with its decaying scenery and rustic remnants of society, a parody of the glittery past, enveloped him. The apocalypse would be tomorrow. There was no lower station for his surroundings to attain.

He returned that year to the public school system.

His final year of high school. Some things came easier at last, not exactly in a manner of improvement, but in that he was a conditioned animal now, conditioned to live off the meager handful of survival tools he was allowed—a dish of water, a few oats, a box of matches, maybe even a hunting knife.

He bumped headfirst into a group of rough girls in the hallway, brandishing nearly enough muscles to corrupt their feminine figure with scowls across the board, possibly they were rugby players. He took a second to inspect them mid-tumble, then kept walking.

"He act like he a senior or somethin'." Snarling behind him, gruff.

"I am," he said, chest puffed out in gleeful triumph, not glancing back, continuing on his only vaguely interrupted path.

He had earned something, some scant rite of passage in return for surviving the horrors of life so long, like the master tossing table scraps to a half starved dog.

He came back to public school by way of his father's discovering a pill on the floor of his room. An orange pill with an M etched at the center, barely standing out from the grey carpet, a soft line of division through the middle of the pill, slicing the M in half. He had never seen it before, or at least did not recall having procured it. He imagined the pill had materialized in the air, floating over the carpet for a second, then dropping down in the forest of dusty fuzz below, awaiting discovery.

Coming into his room just to wake Walter up for schoolchurch, his father spotted it. He clutched Walter by the shoulder and shook him awake.

"What are you on? What are you on?" he roared—the little, orange circle resting in his palm like an oddly colored piece of punctuation at the center of his hand.

"Whuh, what?" Walter stammered, entering wakefulness without a shred of grace.

"What are you on and where are you getting it from?"

"Nothing," he spat out, eyes suddenly open and pupils big as if he *were* high, as if the paranoia of parents could manipulate reality, fear realizing itself right before them.

"Someone at the school. That psycho-religious school, probably full of delinquents. I bet all of them are getting loaded." His palm crushed the pill into dust, sprinkling on the bed beneath them as his fingers unfurled.

Logically, his father's decision made no sense—to force Walter to clean up his act by returning him to public school, like a shepherd thinking the best protection was to toss the sheep that had run away directly into a pack of wolves. Returning him to the school downtown with the catwalk, a cesspool of drug dealers and deviants who had formed a cult around coming school simultaneously high and drunk.

But it worked.

Walter was too shy to interact with anyone around him he didn't know, and he knew virtually no one. He should have known them maybe, the crowd of students with faces vaguely familiar as from an unremembered dream. He could not ask them for substances; he spent most of his time terrified of being noticed.

Mercifully, no one did, no one remembered him or his penis from the incident in the gym. He saw the actual perpetrator once in the hallway and was suddenly frozen in place, recalling the trauma, staring into the boy's face and reliving the horror.

The culprit turned slightly towards him in the hallway while walking, looking at Walter only because he detected the icy mesmerism of the stare directed at him. He returned Walter a confused look, clearly having forgotten him and his penis, continuing on his journey through the teenage infested hallway in the same breath.

Walter stood still, frozen from the eerie memory, someone bumping into him, another one shoving him aside as they passed by.

He snapped from this state gradually, shaking his head and walking on, realizing he had become anonymous. Anonymous—merely another teenage body inhabiting the world but not notably so, a heartbeat beneath his chest you might assume, not memorable for any reason. He was a zombie among the hoard.

He smiled gratifyingly.

He remained drug free for that final year of high school, outside of one instance in the restroom between classes that lasted a foggy hour or so. Coming across the boy who must have stepped out of a Don't Do Drugs infomercial—blood soaked eyes, disheveled hair that looked like there might be some dried glue tangled in the threads, one leg of his jeans with a thigh-sized hole and a joint sloppily hanging from his mouth as an inseparable accessory to his lifestyle.

"Good shit dude," he said, squinting blearily at Walter through his one, currently open eye.

Walter—yet to partake—just having entered the restroom, unzipping his pants and saddling up to a urinal. Several chewed at wads of pink gum collecting at the drain.

"Wanna hit?"

"Sure."

Walter zipped his pants back up without having peed, stepping away from the urinal. He had smelled the marijuana and the possibility of this moment had been what really brought him inside the filthy restroom.

Even based off the modest amount of experience he had at his disposal, Walter knew the second he tasted it that this was not truly *good shit*. But it would suffice in momentarily quelling the ache in him.

Though the inhaling was as dry as swallowing a ball of dust.

He coughed, frowning, while his companion pointlessly erupted into laughter. He never learned the boy's name.

Missing his next class and late to the one after that, Walter tumbled into the classroom, without his book bag—left behind in the restroom perhaps? He was not certain of anything, much less the location of this suddenly unimportant thing.

The teacher spoke directly to him, asking why was he late, perhaps not so friendly as that—was he ready for them to start now?

Each word of the question a bullet, shocking him into his body, here he was and people *did* realize he existed alongside them, breathing their air and participating in the same world they lived and died in.

He preferred anonymity. Maybe he could return to it by shrugging off his teacher's words, settling at his desk as if she had not spoken, reaching for paper to rummage about him, but with none there he awkwardly scraped at the air, then reached into his pocket and found a pen to fumble with.

Someone seated beside him, watching his eyes, asked Walter after class if he had *the hook up*.

He was so touched he wiped at his eyes, feeling the moisture build behind them like a watery heartbeat primed to implode.

He spent his free time playing video games, living in a universe of pixelated screen and sixteen bit sound, a square little man in red and blue plastered over the TV who he could become, a filter for the annoyance of his brain and life outside and anything, anything else.

This was the end of high school. Like everything else before, life continually inflicted on him, perhaps mildly easier but still quite difficult, like being tortured for an eternity and offered a moment to breathe, given a humble meal of rice and beans, half a slice of ham, a break in between the time the eagle devoured his liver.

At least things could not get any worse than they had been; his father was going to send him to college—a shadowed fantasy place of unknowns, where true freedom and autonomy from his present might be obtained.

But could Walter ever trust in the future? If misery had taught him anything, it was that he could not.

Graduation.

The dying breath of high school reared its head and unleashed itself upon him, one final attempt to wipe him out. He was a survivor.

The ceremony waited, gowns and all.

"She called."

His father had interrupted Walter from the jaded thought process drowning him in his room, a Super Nintendo controller in his open palm though the system was shut off.

"Huh?"

"She wants to be there. At your graduation."

Walter dropped the controller and clutched his stomach in his hand, the inside of his body moving independent of him while the outside stiffened, his father returning the existence of her to his mind.

"I know," his father went on. "It's been years since I heard from her."

The well of his twisting stomach. The only thing worse than saying who *she* was to continue referring to *her* by that horrifically mysterious third person pronoun, like *she* was a fleck of sand on the beach, unfindable, drowned by the infinite number of identical brothers and sisters that surrounded her. Saying *she* instead of saying *your mother* was to hammer in what she was until all meaning of that evaporated, to destroy the heart behind the words, like saying *your mother your mother your mother your mother* ad infinitum.

"You should be ready." It seemed his father would never stop talking. "You should be ready to see her."

The window for Walter to respond by some auditory means was there, but went ignored.

He shook his head and tried to look back blankly as if nothing important had been related to him, the return of his mother not a big deal, how could it be a big deal really? Mothers, everyone had them and they went on existing in bodily separation from the person they had once incubated and that was the way of things.

That night spiraling into darkness, squeezing the question into his pillow, conscious behind shut eyelids, mind loosely sketching the last remembered image of her over and over again.

He found the image faded and slipping farther from him all the time. Where was her face in his mind?

Losing consciousness about six a.m. as a trickle of light through the window began to color the shadow of his eyelids grey.

※ ※ ※

Cap and gown itched his skin. Unlike at least one of his peers, he wore clothes underneath.

The boy who was naked was asked to leave quietly behind Walter, a fleck of dirt swept under the rug, everyone whispering about him until a teacher came up and grabbed his armpit and yanked him off.

The end of an era, this strange, clouded phase of Walter's life.

The seventeen- and eighteen-year-olds waited backstage in impatient clusters, mostly avoiding Walter, though he felt vaguely a part of the group, by default, maybe just because of his shared attire, the itchy robe and cap with its droopy tassel.

At last—in alphabetical order—names were called out and each of them emerged on to the stage, to the background echoing of cheering relatives and friends and hokey, forgettable music.

Walter loathed himself for the sentimentality that stirred within his belly. There was something sweet about it, even though he wished to wipe any touch of color from the experience. He looked out on all the people watching, seated about the gymnasium. The same one where school basketball games took place, a net hanging overhead on either side of the room.

He looked for his father in the crowd, Teresa beside him.

His mother wasn't here. He was uncertain why, but did it matter? She had not been around beforehand and she was not here and no potentially filled seat could save the fact that he had ceased to care, or had become so sweetly numb that lack of sensation saved him from disaster.

Another thing he would not have to face. For now.

As he walked across the stage Teresa yowled for him pathetically and his father, alongside her, stared onward blankly.

■ ■ ■

He did not open the sleek, leather binder containing his diploma until they had returned home, his form still awkwardly perched underneath the uncomfortable gown. Sitting in a rocker on the back porch, he shared a cigarette with Teresa, who had become a casual smoker.

He opened the binder, spilling ash across it as he read over the words slowly. In a ludicrous typo, they had omitted the "l" from his name. Water.

He discovered he was silently crying, salty slime traveling down his face. He crushed the almost done cigarette, his hand making a fist around it. The slight burning sensation, there and then not, felt remarkably satisfying.

"What's wrong?" Teresa asked.

"Nothing." He carefully removed the paper from its leather home, folded it, and then ripped it right down the crease.

He dropped the halved paper to the ground, along with

mutilated cigarette, standing up and walking back inside.

His father was seated before the television with characteristic frown, as though not enjoying a second of whatever show his attention was entirely devoted to.

"Dad."

No response—but in a jerky movement, he wiped his nose.

"Dad."

"Yeah."

"Where is she?"

Walter crouched in front of the television, turned it off.

"Tell me."

His father sighed, long and drawn. He looked at Walter dead on. "You don't want to know."

"I need to."

Maybe a curious shred of sympathy leaked into the seriousness of his face. "Are you sure?"

Walter nodded.

"She's in a hospital."

"Why didn't you tell me that?"

"I don't know. I found out right before. The timing wasn't right. It still isn't, really. You just graduated high school."

"I need to see her."

"No ... Walter."

"Take me there." He spread his arms out, grasping at the air.

"It's not close to Wilmington. It would take like four or five hours."

"I don't care where it is. I need to see her."

His father eyed him suspiciously.

"Please."

Everything waited on his father's response, somehow Walter sensing that whatever he said in the next few seconds would be the final answer.

"Alright," he said. "But I'm not going. Teresa will take you."

"Why?" Walter asked, purely curious.

"Because I don't want to see that insane bitch. Get out of the way of the TV." Walter stepped aside and his father lifted the remote.

* * *

The ride was hour after hour achingly stacked on top of each other. The only sound was the road humming underneath them until Walter's bladder at last moved him to speak.

"Stop here," he whispered. "I have to pee."

She offered no verbal answer, but took the exit. Walter felt the vehicle slowing and then stopping.

He opened the car door, stepping out.

Something always had charmed him about the artificiality of rest stops. Like a phony homestead, designed to dupe you into thinking someone might live here, each one identical waiting at another interval along the highway. He loved the ripe, green shade of the grass and how clean the toilets were.

In the handicapped stall, because that was the one he entered, he urinated and then leaned over and vomited into the bowl, blemishing the pure white with the brownish colors of his insides. The feeling of deep, inner discomfort scraping every tender spot along the esophagus as it poured from him and plopped into the water.

He made his way shakily back to the car, wiping his lips, having not touched the sink. Somehow he felt better, as if this *were* the hospital and he had just gone to see her, confronting all of it, memories and pain, instead of just ridding himself of his insides that his body had declined utilizing for hair or energy.

Teresa had not left the car, which she started again.

"Wait," he said.

"What?" she asked flatly, not looking at him, not really halting her effort.

"Why is she in the hospital?"

"Oh," she said, looking down at him like she was a thousand

years older. "I think it's like pneumonia."

"Doesn't sound so bad," he said.

She shrugged. "It probably is. She doesn't exactly take the best care of herself."

The image came to him then—vivid, crisp. The skeleton body pathetically hidden under a white piece of hospital garment, an IV pumping life through her, keeping the idea of her alive, right on the brink of life, enough that if you had to, you could say she was alive.

In the vision. She was not conscious, soft shallow breath the lone clue she was not dead. A doctor carefully explaining to him that she would be fine in a few weeks. To him this seemed the worst part.

"Let's go home," he said, abruptly.

Teresa looked at him, miffed. "But . . . we drove all this way."

"I don't care."

"The hospital is like thirty minutes from here."

"It doesn't matter. I want to go home now."

"Okay," Teresa said. Walter thought her voice had maybe taken on an air of gratitude in that instant.

CHAPTER VII

Pig

College was life inside a flame. Entering, he felt as though the fire would never go out. He applied to only one university and got in— at the other end of North Carolina, nearly as far as he could go from any semblance of what he knew and his father still able to deal with in-state tuition.

A world colored by the overload of sounds all through it.

The girl who lived across from his dorm room smiled at him, unapologetically chubby in her leggings, something shockingly attractive about her (or did he only think so because her attention to him validated him?); his roommate didn't leave the bed for several days in the fit of some ongoing psychedelic nightmare (at least he made little noise other than a meek moan that came and went); the professor who stood on top of a chair and pointed at the ceiling to illustrate a point, to reach a destination where no one followed him, the blank faces of his students seeming to actually flee in the opposite direction; reading the Spark Notes to *Notes From the Underground* for a class and thinking: *This sounds like a really good book—I should actually read this sometime*, but reserving his free time to read the science-fiction/fantasy with slick covers and half-naked, muscled protagonists; waking to his roommate wearing his socks one day and too inhibited to say a word to the drugged out boy about it; the path through the woods and the gardens alongside the dorms, he roamed them, barely a shadow of a tree when by himself; later with the girl who smiled at him, they found a shack of rotting wood and chain smoked Camel Lights as furiously as if they were sweating out their souls; the younger high school boys he met behind the cafeteria one night at three a.m. who corrupted him, their alcohol swishing back and forth inside a twelve-ounce soda bottle, hidden from the adult eye, taunting him in inanimate movement despite astounding power to change the course of his brain.

He turned up the bottle and gulped.

Return of an old friend.

The feeling snaked into him, and behind the cafeteria Walter felt the tickle born in his veins. The warm, hard liquor was a breathing creature inside of him, perhaps an embryo, and he was pregnant.

"Go easy on that," a boy said, the cool-headed one, leaning back on the rail on the handicap ramp that led alongside the steps into the building. The boy was skinny, a presence so slick he didn't have to speak, nimbly twisting back together a Black & Mild cigar he had pointlessly disassembled. He was a character in a movie. After reconstructing the gas station cigar completely, he lit it and began to blow cherry flavored smoke in Walter's direction.

The other boys were more impressed with his knack for chugging hard liquor.

"Wow," said the fat one. His name might have been Grant, or maybe Garret, Walter wasn't sure. "I'm drinking with this guy."

He drank with them until they decided he had drunk enough of their liquor and dispersed without telling him. In his state he was easy to dupe and he turned around realizing he was alone in the darkness with a drop left of the fiery liquid at the bottom of his soda bottle. He finished the liquor off, sitting down on the concreted earth, telling himself they might come back.

■ ■ ■

He lost his virginity at long last in the girl's room in a wriggle of skin and nakedness. The flab of her was beautiful; he lost himself to the wonderful point where he stopped looking for himself anymore.

He felt as though his body became something separate from him that belonged to her. She stroked his penis with the sweetened, loving regard one would save for a pet dog. To feel fingers on it other than his own and to witness the respect she graced him with, he felt the true impossible beauty, he became someone else and merely observed and all was good.

He touched every corner of her body. He lingered at her feet, running his fingers over her toes and soles.

He turned so hard he felt that his penis was tearing itself from that socket of his body where it resided.

He seemed to be at a loss until she gripped him and pulled him into her, uncondomned. His stupid brain was no more; he floated through the organic beauty of her warm insides. Like a plant, a flytrap certainly, swallowing him whole and his not caring a bit, completely aware of the snare.

Less than a minute floating through the bliss he began to make a sound like the soft coo of a bird. Despite the extent of his inexperience with females, he knew what was about to happen. He could feel the end of him rising up and spilling over. He struggled to speak through the lovely stupefaction that had kidnapped him.

"Buh, buh. Betsey."

She opened her eyes and looked at him. His were still closed and he felt deeply drugged, speaking through sabotage.

"I'm going to. Guh, guh going to . . ."

She lifted a finger from his back that had been gliding down the sweaty hill of skin and put it over his gently moving lips. He tasted his own salty water.

"Shhh," she said. "It's okay. Tomorrow I will go buy the pill."

He didn't know what it meant, but he emptied himself before she had even finished saying it. He emptied into her everything that was inside of him, including his memories.

He wouldn't pull out of her, but after a moment she pushed him from her.

He slinked back to her. She put the covers of her bed over them.

Her roommate coughed in the middle of a snore, nearby but invisible in the dark of the dorm room.

He shriveled to a ball of nothing, very near to death. Their naked bodies were glued together now.

Her breath smelled alive, pouring through him like anesthesia. He fell asleep against her breast.

She was awake most of the night, tickling his cheek, breathing on him, whispering to him and herself, as if it were her job to remind them both that they still existed.

■ ■ ■

A pig. He woke up an hour or so later, half wrapped in the belly of a pig, the pink skin dripping over him, wet with scalding sweat that had intermingled with him.

Bestiality. He had fucked a pig.

He was going to be sick.

He had to get away from her.

He untangled himself from the trap of her massive body, rolling from the bed. He touched himself, recalling his own nakedness. He reached towards the bed where he thought his clothes were probably tangled in her sweaty nest, but then he recoiled just as he began to sense her body heat again tickling his skin as he moved closer to her. He darted from the dorm room, naked as if he had been freshly created.

Into the black night he emerged, cold clinging to him, sticking. He seemed not entirely uncomfortable with the punishing temperature; the weather cleansed him, washed him of his disgust a little.

He wished he had a cigarette.

■ ■ ■

At first he didn't drink daily. He drank through the weekend, hard, putting in his order for Aristocrat vodka with a boy everyone called Eminem (after the rapper), who was possibly a heroin addict, scabbed up forearms and all. Eminem wasn't twenty-one yet but had a driver's license with one digit on his birthdate smudged just right to make it appear that he could've been born three years earlier. Eminem wore baggy jeans and had a shaved head and a look to him like he wasn't your friend, or anyone's.

If Walter gave Eminem a twenty, he wouldn't receive any change back.

One Monday, Walter woke up at five a.m. shaking from the night before. His heart felt like an animal seizuring inside his chest.

He wanted to go back to sleep but couldn't.

His brain felt singed with the unmemory and remorse of the night before.

That was when he started purchasing over-the-counter sleeping pills. If he woke up before the sun was up, a handful of them cured him, pulling him back down. They smothered him sweet and slow.

▪ ▪ ▪

He tried the drug in a decision that felt almost accidentally made, but *was* consensual in the end.

A girl he was trying to talk to at a party gave it to him. She kept ignoring his questions and then finally commanded:

"Open your mouth and stick out your tongue."

He did as she asked and felt the plastic melting over his tongue, not knowing what the odd sensation signified.

She smiled at him and ducked into the crowd.

He had a seat by the punch-filled cooler. The punch was half vodka. It swirled about the cooler, a dark red pool of bloody death. Everyone at the party dipped their cups in and gulped the bloody concoction down, like members of a cult partaking in a satanic ritual. He waited by the cooler, sweating, wondering what might happen to him. Had she put death in his body? Did she wish him harm? Her name was Stephanie, dyed black hair, tan skin, barefoot under a long skirt though it was winter, a leaf in the fall drifting through the party, somehow standing out amid the hippie-wannabes that packed the apartment as someone special. Something about how she carried herself. And her face didn't hurt

Walter's eyes either. A face with a secret gleefully kept from you. Intriguing face.

He suspected what was at work inside of him, but for now the walls stayed where they were. She came back.

"What did you give me?" he asked, mostly detached from the discovery.

"Acid." She smiled devilishly. "Come dance with me."

He followed her into the crowd, feeling her skirt brush against him. He noticed her hand on his.

There were too many people to dance, really. Crammed against each other, their bodies moved and swayed a little, possibly to the rhythm of whatever music echoed through the apartment.

Walter removed his elbow from someone's face, apologizing. The guy looked offended, but said nothing, clutching his red nose and melting into the crowd.

Had the drug taken a hold of him yet? Was he any different? He did not think he was any different from the moment before, miraculously untransformed.

"I don't feel it," he said, not sure if he was making an observation or asking a question. He did feel a passive observer, drugged, about to be raped by a drug, having consented to putting the stuff in his body by his dogged attention to the girl, but feeling duped all the same.

"Oh it will take thirty minutes. Sometimes an hour."

This seemed impossible, stupid, defeating the point of doing drugs entirely. Walter was unsure how to feel about acid from his experience thus far.

The party was in a cramped apartment so close to the campus that it could be mistaken for another dorm building. Basically everyone there was an underage student. The room shook with music. All sounds were a blur—voices, music, moans, puking from the bathroom, screams. Was someone screaming?

He wasn't sure. He felt the sticky condensation sizzling from all the bodies huddled together, as if for warmth. He recognized everyone and knew no one.

As Walter moved alongside the girl who had drugged him so readily, he felt that the bass from the music had overridden the room. The bass shook hair on his head, tiny hairs on his arm. The bass shook his insides.

It was as though there was no one in the room, despite being packed, the bass destroying everything else and moving him in a numbing pattern.

He felt the drug coming over him, crushing him, a wave overhead, pushing him into the sand and obliterating his consciousness.

Moving over his mind.

Now it happened.

Now everything around him was breathing, a painting he had been looking at dispassionately on the wall but had, in a flash, gone inside of.

The feeling not entirely pleasant, though there was something pleasant to it, something he couldn't put a finger on.

Actually, as it crawled into him and magnified, the feeling was like pleasure turned up to the point of being unbearable, all his sensations magnified, a baby again—experiencing his magnificent five senses for the first time.

Time passed and things happened and people chattered at him, maybe about him, existing on all sides of him. He forgot time was there.

He looked around.

He was not in the party anymore, he was outside, sitting on the steps of the apartment building, holding his head in one cupped hand. He still felt the thumping bass inside, billowing, shredding his consciousness.

He looked up. Penciled-in, grey eyes were on him, had been studying him—for how long he was not sure.

In front of him was the most beautiful girl he had ever seen.

He had seen her before, years ago.

Katherine.

Her elegant chin held his gaze like a magnet.

"Hello Walter," she said.

"Kuh, Katherine? I mean, Kat."

She nodded. She was smiling. She was older of course, even more womanlike now but still possessing the perfect touch of girlishness in her smile. She was in a springtime dress though it was winter and they were outside in the cold night. The flowers on her dress contracted and expanded, softly, gently. They seemed to rub Walter's eyes soothingly.

"Yes, yes. It's me." Her smile grew golden.

"I, I don't believe it. How could you be here?"

She reached out and picked lint from her flowery dress. "I live here now." She said it as though she was comforting a child, the most obvious information in the world.

He looked from her to the palm of his open hand for a moment, the wrinkled skin on it warping under his drugged scrutiny—a pink, twirling spiral. He jerked it away from his face and looked back to her. "Acid doesn't make you see things like this," he told himself out loud. "You are so vivid. You're real."

"I'm real," she said, laughing. Her face was crisp, detailed. Not the product of drugs, even if the flowers that melted across her dress might have been. "What are you doing here? I recognized you from over there. You looked so strange sitting on those steps. Are you okay?"

"I go to the university." He pointed in front of them, but it wasn't even mildly in the direction of where he went to school.

"Did you say you were on acid?" She looked slightly concerned.

"Yes," he said. Maybe he shouldn't tell her about the acid, he decided then. "I mean, no. I had a bunch of the punch though."

"But you said you thought you could be seeing things. The punch doesn't do that."

"Yeah, okay, maybe I might be on acid, a little."

Her face went white. "That's intense. Do you do stuff like that a lot?"

"Not really. This girl just gave it to me."

"Are you okay?"

He felt his insides stir, nausea too deep-rooted to come up in puke. He had to defend himself. "I'm fine! I'm fine! Having a blast." He smiled, big and toothy and ludicrous.

"Okay, if you say so."

"Anyways, anyways. You're here! You stepped right out of my past."

She continued to look back at him uneasily. "Yes! I moved to this apartment complex last year with my fiancé," she explained. "I used to go to school there too, but I dropped out when I got pregnant last year."

"Boy or girl?"

"Her name is Alicia. She's a few months old now."

With her words, she grew horribly older to him. Time sped up, leapt forward, moving with violent speed. He stifled a scream from spilling out of him.

"I have to go," he said.

"Wait," she said. "I haven't seen you in a long time. We should get lunch some time or something."

"I'm sorry," he said. "I'm sorry. I have to go. I hope to see you again." He stood up from the steps.

He started walking away. He didn't look for her gaze but was certain it was on him, heavily.

By the time he reached the road, he heard police sirens behind him. The party was getting busted, good that he had left.

Or were the drugs blending up the mush of his mind?

He couldn't be sure; the sirens went away so fast it could have been his imagination in a heartbeat.

He lay awake on his dorm bed the entire night, sleep not crawling into his body for a second, the acid fast-forwarding his thoughts into a bright, messy unorganized pile of useless shit. Darting in and out of his head like lost children running for their lives.

He quietly wished he had not put the thing in his body and acknowledged that it had stolen the last shred of control over himself he had.

CHAPTER VIII
Masturbating Quietly

The year he dropped out of college and moved back to the beach, the world turned hot, the seasons mirroring a similar change in the pit of his stomach. Spreading through him, merciless, tearing the old him to shreds was the past inside, burning.

Twenty-one.

Society said he was a man by now, but he suspected he was merely a full grown animal. Eating and shitting and masturbating, quietly, after his dad went to sleep at night. He could be done in two minutes or less, had the act down and performed it as few times as possible. Twice a week, a practice he did not entirely enjoy but did out of respect for his body. Like eating his greens or exercising.

The kitchen table was sticky with the mark of microscopic life. Walter sat there, trying not to let his elbow, or a molecule of his skin, graze the surface of the table. He ate as delicately as he could, lifting his fork from his plate like an antique ceramic doll that would shatter in his hands.

They were eating leftover crockpotted chicken, the only dish his father prepared with confidence.

His father's plate was untouched, the chicken's skin peeling up in a grey, sick-looking curlicue.

"Was it worth it?"

By now Teresa long gone, the house empty but for the hollow echo of his father's discontent. The house reeked of masculine resentment. The place barren like desert land, each room stretching over the horizon line, to walk from one end to the other when alone in the room could take hours—water breaks included, socked feet tumbling forward.

"Do you know how much money it was?" His father picked up the fork beside his plate, put it down.

The downtown neighborhood had turned uglier in the years. One way up the street was a church with a rickety sign installed outside the yard, *REPENT* with a dangling "T." On the other side of the street was the ghetto, a world Walter had only peeked at, a place that—just by being there—dared him to stand anywhere near and be comfortable, and be himself in the midst of this place that his fear told him he could not relate to, never in a thousand years. He heard a gunshot or two at night, singling itself out in the silent, nonreactive dark.

"Thousands. Thousands of dollars just for you to live there, eat and drive around." His father's hand had snuck into the plate of food and was resting over the lumpy chicken skin.

Another block or so would bring you into familiar downtown area, still tourist-ridden and the high school where he once dated a witch looming by the street. Coffee shops and gag stores abounded.

"That's not even the money for the school." His fingers stretched around the chicken skin, clutching, squeezing. A grease bubble popped over his hands, a thought flickering out forever. Underneath his palm a white puddle oozed.

The world was empty except for him and his father. With no school, no college, no girl, nothing but the two of them made any difference. And they didn't make any difference.

"I'm in debt, Walter." He pulled his hand out of the food, inspecting the palm, with the other hand picking a string of chicken from it. He looked back up at him. "When are you getting a job?"

Walter put down his fork, half-bitten food hanging from his mouth. He looked at his father.

He shrugged.

Words were not sufficient; they'd had this argument before. Waiting out the tirade was Walter's single option.

And he didn't have the patience.

He stood up in his chair, his silverware clanking at the table, his chair pushed aside by the movement, squeaking against the tile floor. He looked at his father a long time before turning around.

His father opened his mouth, clearly about to speak and then closed it without having spoken.

Walter walked away. He slid into his tennis shoes and went out the front door into the street.

Seven p.m. and the outside was flickering into dark. The sun still hung, orange and unthreatening, coloring the world briskly. The roads called Walter—he moved towards them without shutting the door. Before he had made it out of the driveway, the light fallen through the doorway blinked out. His father shutting the door behind him, wordless.

Walter walked along the road, almost achieving a blankness in himself, a numbness that rubbed out all. In that painless place but not quite—the edges of his world were dully colored with pain. The pain of the casualness with which his father had closed the door. He imagined it would be a pleasant surprise for him not to return before night hit.

Though he would, of course.

But most of him was that placid, nudging numbness, God's gift, dark and cold, digging through his body, burying itself, conquering him without prejudice, without taking notice, just plowing through him.

He was fodder to the numbness.

He walked down the center of the road. He felt there was not another road, or another direction, or anything other than his feet following each other through the darkened neighborhood.

Downtown fell around his eyes. Entering downtown was an event, forcing itself on you at all times. Seven p.m. on a Wednesday was no exception. People tumbled across the road, pushing through each other, college children laughed, drunkards spoke over each other, cars waited for the light to turn green.

He plodded through, he wanted to put his hands on a young boy, stupid, clumsily wobbling in front of him. The boy had on a red hoodie and a baggy pair of jeans, his hair obnoxiously gelled, gleaming blond, shining without the aid of the light. The boy shouted, intoxicated. Walter wanted to put his hands on the boy, not to steady him or to shake sense into him. Walter wanted to put hands on him and throw him into the street and keep walking as he listened to the cars squashing his intoxicated squeals.

Walter didn't do things like that, he never had. He just thought them, searing thoughts scorching his mind leaving charcoaled pieces, leaving scars that came back up. Trying to forget they were there was the best way to cope.

He came to the coffee shop where the girl worked and started to go in. Then he stopped himself, hand on the door. He took two steps back and too many thoughts invaded his mind, right when he'd been so close to achieving that sweet numbness.

What if she isn't there?
What if she is though?
What will I say to her?
What reason do I have to buy coffee at seven o'clock?

He deliberated for three more beats of his heart, counting them, wishing he didn't still care about girls. If only he had been gay. How much easier life would have been had he been gay. Well, probably not—when they had called him faggot the word stung for that many more years, the truth crushing his soul to bits. *You are different than us*, the truth screamed at him.

He *would* go in the coffee shop; she wasn't working now—she worked in the mornings. Her name was Kiwi. That's what her little nametag said, etched in silver letters across the black rectangle of plastic above her breasts. How could her name be Kiwi? It was a joke, that was not her name. She had made that nametag herself, or a friend, or someone being completely unserious, daring to make a joke.

He didn't know for sure, it could be her name, he had never asked her. He had never had the courage to say anything more than, "I'd like a mocha. Tall."

Still, he told himself that she recognized him sometimes, that some flash of color behind her eyes betrayed a secret pleasure at finding him in front of her again.

Her skin with that consistent freckling, that mysterious tilt to her eyes, slits on her face, the smile of her killed him. She looked foreign, Asian, certainly but what? Korean? Japanese? Then there was something plain old Caucasian about her too; her hair was nearly red.

She was pretty, but not too much. She was probably twenty, but had some of the mannerisms and features of a thirty-year-old woman. There was something refreshingly trashy about her, she smelled like cigarettes and her voice had an unhealthy rasp.

He breathed out, relieved, when she wasn't the barista at the counter, instead greeted by a safely unattractive girl with frizzy hair, older than he, possibly even thirty. She chewed gum, viciously devouring it in the side of her cheek, and her eyes had a deadly uninterested look to them. He felt safe around her, wonderfully safe. Her nametag said, *Heather*.

What a perfectly safe name.

"Can I help you?" Somehow she asked this reasonable, polite question in a tone of utter rudeness. Also her cheek continued to chomp at her gum as she spoke, not a drop of saliva spilling.

"A mocha," he said. "Tall."

Heather didn't say anything, but her brown eyes bore through him, not watching him, as the rest of her body went to work at the register, taking two dollars from his hand, and then moving alongside the register and fiddling with the espresso machine as she set about materializing his drink. Still not breaking the unwatching eye contact.

A question bubbled at his throat, he didn't want to ask, wasn't entirely sure what it was, the fear in him tried to pin his inquisitiveness back down, to stop the words from coming. But they poured out. The vomit of his soul.

"Is Kiwi working tonight?" he heard himself ask.

The methodical process of espressoing halted midway, Heather looked at him, actual expression dangerously invading her dull look.

"Kiwi huh?" she said skeptically.

That's what her nametag says, Walter was about to say, but he choked back the statement.

"Yeah she's here." The frizzy-haired girl slammed his mocha in front of him on the counter. A brownish dollop sloshed down the side. "She's taking a break."

Walter wrapped his fingers around the cup, watching the suds of coffee ooze toward his skin. "Oh," he said. "Will she be back soon?"

"She'd better be," Heather said. She turned her back on him, having something to do at one of the coffee machines behind the counter, going at it voraciously.

Walter watched Heather attack the coffee machine, a mini-tower of steel, rattling and whizzing.

He walked off, feeling his fingers turn warm where the espresso dribble now touched them, heading out of the coffee shop. He stopped though, right after going out the door. Someone bumped into him even though he wasn't quite in the street yet. He spilled a little mocha on himself, but not much.

He looked down his shirt and rubbed at the new wet spot. This did nothing to remove the moisture from his clothes, permanent and looking back up at him, darker than the rest of his stupid, pale blue shirt. He pinched the spot between two fingers, picking at it.

He looked up from his shirt, through the glass doors, saw her replacing Heather behind the counter. The red hair, the dark, half-hidden eyes.

No job, no place to live of my own.

What do I have to lose?

He went back into the coffee shop.

■ ■ ■

"So your name is really Kiwi then?" he asked, stupidly, as awkward after sex as he had been before. In her bed. Her room was messier than his back at his father's house. Strewn clothes looking several times worn, a shag green carpet peeking out from the rubble like a massive, sleeping moss-creature, the mew of a cat he had yet to see that never went longer than five minutes without invading their solace.

Under the bed, he grabbed his boxers and shoved himself back into them, feeling safer not to be naked.

She in her bare body—twisting alongside him, stretching and yawning.

Now that he had seen her, she was twice as imperfect. She had a beer gut. She had tan lines despite the overall olive shade of her that contrasted his papery whiteness.

She had two moles beside each other on her back, muddy eyes staring back at him, impassive.

"Yeah, no shit Sherlock," she said. She turned off the lamp nearby, dousing the faint red light over them, briefly flicked on to satisfy the late night urge. She closed her eyes and dug her face into his armpit, hiding from him in his own body.

He felt the rhythm of her breath changing in seconds, watching her consciousness diving into the deep end.

I wish I could go to sleep like that, he thought.

He snapped his eyes shut with uncomfortable force, attempting to shove himself into sleep.

At least forty minutes passed.

He had a difficult time sleeping with a girl in the bed, something he relearned every time (this was the third).

He had a difficult time sleeping at all, the thoughts in his head an enemy, a disease that ate him alive but a disease that kept him alive at the same time, kept him continuing, trying.

Suddenly something ran over top of him, tickling him, imposing the existence of itself on him out of nowhere in the dark.

He reached out and heard the yarl of the cat.

His hand darted back to his side as if bitten. He waited in the dark, not sleeping.

The next morning she made eggs, not particularly for him. The sizzle of them stung the air, grease, a powerful stench, an invasion of the coming day to smell something so strong in his half-wakened state. He rubbed at his tired eyes, hoping to wipe them clean without showering, hoping to think himself awake.

He reached into his pocket and pulled out the battered little flip phone, placing it on the table. The phone was buzzing with unchecked text messages, undoubtedly from his father. This was the first night he hadn't come home, other than the night he got black out drunk and passed out in a high school friend's backyard, mid-piss. He turned the phone off.

"Goddamn it Dad," he muttered.

"What's that?" she said, looking back from her eggs.

"Nothing," he said. "Just—my dad. I don't really want to go back there."

Kiwi shrugged her shoulders, her back to him. "Then don't."

Walter raised his eyebrows.

"I mean, I'm not saying stay here. But you could like get a job somewhere, get your own place."

"Where do I stay until then? I don't want to go back."

"Oh Jesus, kid. You're how old again? "

"Twenty-one."

She snickered over the darting grease of the eggs, her back to him still. She had a cigarette in her mouth, he realized as he watched the profile of her. Turning herself, just barely, to almost face him. To face the direction of him. The cigarette, unlit, between her lips waiting to be set on fire.

"Twenty-fucking-one."

She put eggs down. Sat down across from him. He watched the wrinkles in her face. "Well how old are you?"

She lit the cigarette over her plate of eggs, almost certainly spilling ash into it as she took the first drag. Smoking was like a part of the meal, as important or more so. The cigarette seemed to have been prepared in the same sense that she had prepared the eggs.

"I'm twenty-nine," she said, smoke popping in and out of her lips as she spoke through the cigarette.

Walter looked down at the eggs and picked them up with two of his fingers (forkless) and started to eat.

He swallowed and the food moved through him, in collaboration with his body.

"You can stay here kid," she said through a yellowy mouthful. "Probably. I just got to ask my boyfriend if it's okay first. Sometimes he stays here, but usually he's on the street." She paused, perhaps thinking or perhaps chewing. "I need to talk to him today anyways."

Somehow this was spoken so casual that there was nothing wrong, nothing surprising about the situation. This had not been hidden, simply something Walter had not known until the moment she spoke it.

"What's his name?" Walter asked, purely curious.

"He doesn't exactly have one," Kiwi said, swallowing. "I call him Fuckio."

■ ■ ■

Walter had his hands inside his pockets, rubbing the linen between his fingers, his overworn jeans carrying him through downtown.

He followed Kiwi shyly, a butterfly trailing a darty mosquito. Kiwi weaving through sidewalks and alleys, barely seen at that pace, her body a better vehicle for travel than a car or a bicycle, ripping through downtown Wilmington. Walter clumsily dancing behind. She smoked another cigarette as she went, the cloud tailing behind her, like she was burning up fuel and expelling the fumes.

Walter saw downtown from an angle he never had before. He walked down streets he might have been down three days ago and this seemed his first time encountering them. Road names he hadn't noticed, *Princess Street*, what a ludicrous storybook name, named by a child maybe; the pocket in a brick wall in the corner of an alleyway housing a pigeon still as God, not a single feather betraying its sentience; the bricked graffiti telling a story in colorful mythology, though the implication was destroyed in an expletive or the perverseness of the delivered punch line.

The people in this area of town he had never really noticed before. Before, they seemed locked away, or not worth getting to know, empty faces and eyes like holes in their heads showing their hollowness. Now they looked dirty and interesting, older, mysterious. A homeless man slumped where two brick walls met, no longer looking at him as an easy mark but with a friendly look, very nearly a smile entering the crust of his chipped at face. A man in a suit walked by, offering him an astute nod, brisk but unmistakable, or did he imagine the nod?

When the two of them had walked through twenty minutes of downtown, the buildings became vacant, boarded, the graffiti darker, more grisly, rising about them like bloody clouds—the coming of war before the rain stained them red.

They went inside a building with a smiling mouth painted in mid-cackle, lips big and red and lipsticked, teeth glinting white bone. The opening they entered—doorless.

The smell was like having chalk shoved in your nose.

Walter tried not to look around, scared suddenly, realizing the building was not empty. A grown woman rolled around underneath him, mumbling to herself. There were several men in the corner, twitching erratically. One had no clothes on, his chest a pink skeleton. The kind of place that entering required you to leave your soul at the door. The building had a stone-cold attitude that refused to as much as shrug at him in acknowledgement, simply leaving him with a sense that it watched and was aware. He stepped over a random board with several nails protruding.

Walter continued to follow Kiwi, cautiously stepping over the bodies, audible voices rising from them, heated whispers, in argument with themselves.

They came to the largest room yet. The floor here was strangely bare of vomit and people. At the front was a toilet, resting on the tile floor and unconnected by plumbing, and a small battery-operated television on a box. A young man, shirtless but wearing holed jeans, sat at the filthy-looking toilet. Walter recognized him instantaneously.

"Fuckio!" Kiwi squealed. She darted across the room and threw her arms around him.

He batted her away. "Get off. *Seinfeld* is on. I can be your Fuckio in thirty minutes."

Walter opened his mouth and closed it. He opened it again. "I know you?"

The young man seemed to notice Walter, the presence of him bleeding the air, Walter displaced against the sheer comfort of his secure slouch over the toilet seat.

Though the recognition was already there, Walter examined the agedness of him. He had created his own world and only in that world did he exist.

To acknowledge his existence at all, Walter knew he must enter that world too. Like stepping into the lion's den to say hello. A dangerous prospect.

The man's face glaring, expressionless but filled with all the horrible things that could happen to a person. He looked on at other people as if they were from another species, disinterested, not relating to them and not interested in doing so.

This was the face of apathy—of indifference to all the pain contained inside and outside.

His personality erased for the sake of the symbol of him. Would a wrinkle tell you the secret of his age? Was he born a hundred years old? Had he been born? If he had a mother, the emptiness of this expression never betrayed the knowledge of her existence. An orphan.

His mustache was crafted of slime, perhaps dirt over his face that had, itself, sprouted hair. Or maybe a greasy bald man tore the last hairs from his head and wiped them right above the mouth. The slimy thing curled now at the edges as he had allowed the slick light hairs to grow. He had a light beard now to match. His skeleton chest was bare in the sunlight coming in through the unshuttered window.

"Smiley?" Walter asked hopefully.

"How do you know that name?" Smiley's slimy mustache twisted halfway into his mouth, about to eat the thing off his face.

"I met you when I was a kid. On the beach."

Smiley chewed at his 'stache, sucking the grease.

"Hardly anyone calls me that these days." Smiley frowned, deep and meaningful.

"What do they call you?" Walter asked. He watched Kiwi out of the corner of his eye. She had slouched alongside Smiley and was rubbing his chest, her arms moving across him. She was now watching the TV, though Smiley wasn't really anymore.

"Different things. Depends on how I know them."

"This is Walter," Kiwi said. She was crouching now, huddled alongside Smiley, beneath him subserviently. Her skinny arm moving through the hairs of his chest with the gracefulness of an Olympic swimmer treading water.

Smiley's face twisted, studying Walter. Then he allowed himself a flicker of a smile, for a second, and whipped his attention back to the tiny television.

"I remember you now," he said. "You drank almost all my vodka, on the beach."

Walter nodded.

"I thought you were going to throw up your organs that day."

"I don't drink anymore," Walter said nervously, looking down, being asked a very difficult question to which the answer was closely monitored and graded.

"Oh yeah?" Smiley eyed him, allowing perhaps a trace of curiosity into his face. "Going to those double-A meetings er somethin'?"

Walter watching his feet. "Sometimes. Sometimes those just make me want to drink more."

"Hmm."

"Walter's gonna stay with me for a while Fuckio," Kiwi said. She stood up, slowly.

"Sure, whatever."

"Do you have anything for him to do? He's kind of hopeless."

"Maybe," Smiley said.

His smile came back. Walter knew why they had started calling him that; he had a smile like the devil. "There might be a thing or two I could use him for around here."

There was a loud sound outside, deafening. The sound not even mildly diverting Smiley's attention to the rerun of *Seinfeld*.

In fact, no one in the entire building jumped except for Walter. The sound might have been a gun firing, but Walter wasn't sure he would recognize a gunshot if he heard one.

His cell phone buzzed in his pocket a single time, a bug that returned relentlessly after being swatted away.

He pulled it out of his pocket and snapped it in half in one motion.

CHAPTER IX
Become a Body

Debauchery.

He drew it up about him like a crusty blanket left over from childhood, stained with urine. It kept him warm and safe.

Living in these conditions became a disgusting comfort. A home could be found here, a deliciously dilapidated one where he was not judged, not even noticed. He moved through the turning bodies, invisible, invincible. Each one of them a breathing skeleton, incapable of doing him harm. If they reached out to grasp at him, their fingers would shatter, glass dropped on the floor.

Smiley handed him a sweaty wad of bills every few days in exchange for all he did. Smiley seemed to have no concept of money, maybe likely to burn a hundred dollar bill as he was to pass it through his hands into Walter's. Like he could do both these things in the space of two hours and not see a difference between them. Despite this, Smiley continued to accumulate funds.

Usually the chores Walter ran for him were not drug related. But sometimes they were. Such a thing came with the territory.

He carried a zip-locked handful of the tannish white powder in his pocket at least five times. Simply powder, some fake smack to shut up an especially clamoring resident, raising a fuss, disturbing the perfect balance of driveling zombies, sleeping away the nightmare of life on their side, drooling puke onto the tile floor underneath them.

There was violence. Walter never saw a gun but was aware of the close presence of them. Either he was an idiot (which he was definitely not) or Smiley had one somewhere, probably tucked away in the wall of his room where he kept all the hundred dollar bills, next to the fluffy pink insulation behind the walls, contrasting the nature of the room with the insulation's cotton candy look, recalling a flashy memory of the circus from childhood.

For the most part, and sometimes disappointedly, Walter missed out on the violence. He ran boring errands for Smiley, buying his food because he hated to buy anything himself, cleaning up the vomit out of a room that had begun to smell too pungent.

He suspected most of the violence came at night and he spent most of his nights sleeping—mostly on the couch now—at Kiwi's.

One time he was cleaning the vomit beneath a man who appeared still from sleeping. When he peeled one string of bile that clung to the man's cheek in between the collapsed cave of his lips, Walter had the intuition to hold an ungloved hand in front of that cave and feel for the heat of his breath.

None came.

He stepped back for a second and examined the body. He saw the leathery hand sprouting a disorganized smattering of filthy fingers. The hand rested on the chest as if in sleep, as if the chest would rise and fall with each breath taken. One finger on the hand was shriveled up around the black nail, it had been reduced, shorter than the other fingers.

He once had the thought that everyone here was basically a body. He had the thought to join them, to find a needle somewhere to plunge into his own arm, his own vein, and wait to die happily alongside them. And become a body.

Now, the first definite body he encountered, the first one entirely uninhabited by animation, he was afraid.

He nearly forgot about fear since finding Kiwi and refinding Smiley, adopting their courage for his own. Not courage, more like a strong impassivity within that could not be uprooted.

But for him this had been a mask, a flimsy costume now peeling from him. He was not as strong as they were. He was a creature of fear and had been since the day he was born, twenty-two years prior to that moment.

Today was his birthday—August 19, 2007. Twenty-two years ago he had been born. To what purpose? His life was tolerable finally, but continued to strike him as a joke played on him by the universe.

He gave in to the fear. Running through the building, traces of vomit-saliva on his hands.

He stepped on someone somewhere—the person did not cry out but rolled over under the fury of his tennis shoe, almost tripping him.

Walter staggered out of the drug house, pouring into the street.

Early afternoon and the street was bustling with people by the time he was two blocks to downtown.

▪ ▪ ▪

Cars honked at him as he crossed the street. They were a movie in front of him that he paid no attention to, unimportant despite the connection they had to his life and the respect he'd had in the past for their power to destroy him.

His uncle had died from the swerving car of a drunk driver. Not that it was important. He had never known his uncle well enough and the only thought he had been able to think at the funeral was this: *Uncle Ralph sure smelled bad.*

He traipsed across the road, diving into a nearby shop.

Alternative clothes for trapping tourists. Orange and purple and brown ultra-thin cloth dangled around him, tickling him, faintly touching him, an old woman's crippled hand reaching out and grazing his cheek.

He pushed his way through the store, almost bulldozing a meek clerk who was stocking dresses.

"Can I help you sir?" The clerk looked him up and down.

Walter stopped moving. Looking up, returning from the daze. "May I use the bathroom?"

The clerk raised his chin, as if—though he was shorter than Walter—he was looking down at him. "The restrooms are for paying customers only."

"I'm going to buy something," Walter lied, "—just let me piss first." He realized how hard he was breathing, in recovery from his stomping through the dusty streets. Each brick a thousand years old and having been through more than he ever had.

The clerk stared at him.

Walter realized he smelled like the dead and the drugs they had clung to until entering that state. The price paid for the greatest things in life: life.

"Get out of my store."

"But—"

"I will call the police." His lips pursed like a woman.

Walter reversed his direction and moped out, not even needing to urinate, not even sure why he felt defeated again.

He wandered, head down, utterly done for, not sure where he was going but not surprised when he found himself at Kiwi's.

He tried the door. Locked.

Sat on the steps, hands bunched up over his knees, waiting. Waiting was what he had always done—his primary weapon against the disaster that inevitably attacked him.

She did not come.

People walked by. A boy carrying a deflated basketball with a contorted, angry look on his face. An enormous woman—with thousand-year-old, sagging ebony skin—pushing a stroller, inside a pale baby curiously looking around. The baby was confused, the world had betrayed him and he had not reached a point yet where betrayal was a thing that made any sense. A troop of mischievous teenagers, eyes darting, busy talk between them, conspiring to take over the world.

An unbelievable amount of time passed, and he was motionless.

■ ■ ■

Night. He was in a movie that had been in color and faded into black and white. The dull grey black sneaking about him, creeping into the world, somehow the evolution subtle. Never a chaotic invasion, never abrupt. The most covert act of nature, night, this twelve-hour occurrence. Happening around him, never *to* him, not like the way rain could come and conquer sun, just devouring, claiming the world for its own and soaking every human in sight.

The coldness of it so powerful, so animal. He could be dead and nothing different would happen.

He rose from his stationary stance, slow, emerging from sludge. He walked around the corner of the house. Looking up, he studied the open window above his head, Kiwi's warm bed hiding behind. He put a hand to the brick, feeling chunky, ancient skin, gritty pieces peeling into his palm as his fingers tried to curl around it to grasp something.

Beside him was a tree. He looked up and saw a thin branch tickling the shade on Kiwi's window. He turned to the tree, slapping himself against its leathery body. His attempt to scale was instantly impossible.

He had forgotten how to climb a tree.

Had he ever known though?

He re-taught himself as quickly as he could, or at least discovered how for the first time. He did the most pathetic and least successful of pull-ups, half-propelling himself with a tennis shoe to the bark, wrangling his way atop the closest and thickest branch to the ground. Above him dangled the stick that touched the shades. He reached out and it snapped off in his hand. Holding the little thing, he looked at it for a moment. Then he reached for the window and grasped the edge of the window frame in his hands. He yanked himself up and inside.

He spilled through the shades and into the bedroom, one shade coming with him, an assortment of tangled, clumsy sounds.

There was a smell like earth mixed with human skin in the room.

The lights were out and there was the unheard sound of breathing, maybe more of a feeling than a sound. He slunk from his clothes and slithered on top of the bed sheets. He sensed the body next to his and resisted the urge to curl up around it.

He slid into sleep, sneakily, sleep a place he had to go but was not allowed in, a place he had to fool into thinking he belonged there.

He waited in the blackness, happy to be unaware again of the insanity that was around him, also waiting. Patiently.

In his unconsciousness, he heard the body beside him sigh or snore or just become vaguely aware for a half-second.

                        ■ ■ ■

His eyes separated themselves in the sunlit room. He blinked at the yellow blur before him.

The world became details. The cat on the dresser, a Q of sleek black fleece appearing wet from the glisten. The sea of rising and falling bed sheet wrinkles. Rising to a mountain beside him.

The sepia tone shadow of the drapes dulled the hairy brown tentacle resting by his face, disguised it enough that the furry tentacle took a moment to register. The fur grazed his nose smelling of dirt and grease. Noticing, he twitched away.

He rolled from the alien body in the bed. The fur-tentacle was actually a dread hanging from the messy freckled girl, looking about his age, twitching in her sleep.

Walter moved carefully now, conscious of each breath he took, sensing some dangerous possibility watching him, uncertainty dangling. The future—even the very near future—was not something he could put his finger on anymore.

He rolled out of the bed as deftly as he could. He looked for his clothes at the floor and finding them, slowly wrapped them back around him.

He looked at the dreaded girl, still softly breathing. He felt danger but didn't know what kind, and somehow fear left him, almost always a part of him in the real presence of what *could* happen, the fear slithered out of him, hardening once reaching the air and falling away, dead skin flaking off. The sleek pink new body underneath emerged.

He stood closer, sniffing the dirty air around her. He waited for whatever was going to happen to happen.

It didn't.

The silence happened, the unmoment, the nothing hovered. He leaned in closer to her, smelling her dirtied skin, watching her dreadlocks as if they were independent entities about to move on their own, about to writhe and spasm.

Nothing happened.

He reached out a finger and touched a dread. To his skin it was more like slime than hair, more like something from the sea than a creature of fur. The grease came off on his fingers. He wiped his hands on his pants.

Nothing happened

He wanted to go a step further, but wouldn't allow himself.

Over the course of the next ten seconds, his curiosity won and he lightly grabbed the bed sheet which stopped at her neck, covering most of her in the thin wrinkly linen, and he gingerly peeled the sheet back, slowly—

Underneath she had on a bikini top and ratty denim shorts, cut-offs with dangling string. Her stomach was flat, taut, he observed. Her hands clutched a gleaming metal thing he admired with not enough respect for its power. His insides tingled at the sight. He reached.

She moaned and rolled over and moaned and her eyelids flickered.

Her eyelids flickered back shut and he was about to reach again when her voice came. Monotone, droll. Unconcerned.

"Who the fuck are you," she said.

The shock that she was awake (and that maybe his inability to resist his own curiosity had caused this) disabled his answering. He tried and failed to find the fear again, in hope that it would sharpen his senses.

One of the eyes opened. He saw the pupil was massive, a black void. The iris around was green.

"Are you the boyfriend she calls Fuckio?"

Having expected death he was too shocked still to respond, recovering himself, frantically searching for an option.

Both her eyes slammed open and her other hand slapped around the gun and her arms rose, carrying it in his direction.

He stared down the barrel.

"Answer me. Motherfucker."

He felt urine in his pants. His old friend fear, returned, only having gone for a moment.

He swallowed his voice. And then couldn't figure out why words wouldn't come when he opened his mouth. Finally, at the same time as imagining he heard a click, he shook his head, remembering he still had the power to respond with his body, which was not entirely frozen.

"Yeah," she said, lowering the barrel and surveying him. She had propped herself up on her elbows. "You're too chicken shit to be him."

She was lighting a cigarette now. Walter wasn't sure where the cigarette had come from, or the lighter. He wasn't sure if he had lost a few minutes in time. His pants felt sticky and already the smell was overwhelming.

"Little guy like you," she sneered. "The fuck are you even doing in here? Hasn't been anybody since I did the bitch in."

Walter started to open his mouth, then closed it. He smelled the acidic air of her cigarette. Despite the situation, he found himself wanting one too.

Her dreads shook as she spoke between puffs. "How old are you kid?"

"Twenty-two." He found himself able to talk, perhaps due to the mundane nature of the question, the simple natural reflex of answering such a question was comforting, familiar.

"Yeah. Well. What are you doing here?"

"I, I, I—"

She laughed and her dreads shook. "Relax. I'm not going to shoot you. Have a cigarette." She held out a menthol Camel. The little green line running around the white cylinder matched her eyes. Walter snatched it greedily, instantly, stuffing the cigarette in his mouth and sucking away, already trying to smoke without having lit the other end.

She passed him a Zippo lighter with a hologram of a naked woman on it. He could just barely register the absurdity of this in his mind as he snapped the lighter open and used it to light his menthol, breathing in the minty fumes, tasting like toothpaste that shoved itself down his throat and scratched up his gullet.

"So. What are you doing here kid? I do need to know."

He took a deep drag and felt his mind whirl through the events of recent weeks and all the different approaches he could or should take to the question. Truth? Lie? He wasn't even sure that he would know the difference after hearing either one come out of his mouth.

"Um. Uh. I sleep here sometimes. With Kiwi. I ran away from my dad's a couple weeks ago. I don't have anywhere else to go."

She crinkled her brow at him, tossing the rest of the sheets off and sitting up now. Her expression was not unfriendly, but concentrated on him, devouring him. "Maybe you can help me."

He gulped the scratchy smoke down and coughed for a beat of his heart. "I'll try," he managed to choke out.

"Do you know who this Fuckio is?"

He spent too much time thinking about the question before answering. "No," he said.

Her expression went from mildly half-friendly to suddenly cross. "You're lying."

She stood up from the bed, he saw that she was a head taller and striking in her Amazon ferocity. Her body was feminine and shapely muscled, looming, holding the gun. Her other hand ripped the cigarette out of his mouth and pushed him, hard.

He tumbled back against the dresser. Her hands were slimy, dirty. One of them was wrapped around his throat. He wasn't sure which one, he wasn't sure if she still had the gun in her hand or she had dropped it. He thought maybe she had set it down for a moment and his eyeballs darted around, but they couldn't see anything.

They saw her face.

Her eyes cornered his, forcing him to look at her. He felt the grime of her finger slapped around his throat. He could breathe fine for the moment but sensed that this was entirely in her control.

"I gave you a cigarette and you're lying to me."

He tried to talk again and couldn't.

"You're lying to me you, you little dickless fuck. You're not worth anything to me. What makes you think you can tell me anything other than the stone cold truth and I won't put a hole in your goddamn head?"

The other hand holding the gun. He saw it now. That hand waving the gun around, deliriously displaying its presence, hovering nearby, present, waiting to take his life.

She dangled her gun hand drunkenly by her face, lolling the weapon about. "What makes you think I haven't done this before? What makes you think you can lie to me? What makes you think I haven't killed at least five people before?" She paused, presumably for the dramatic effect, which was entirely lost on Walter, whose fear was much louder than her monologue. "Well, I mean, one of those *was* a team effort, and I don't know for sure if the person was dead, but none of us ever saw him again and his car went off the road—"

There was a sound that was more of a vibration inside of everything, including Walter's head. The gun she was waving around had gone off. Walter wondered if he was shot, if he would know for sure that it had even happened. Or if he would find out later, bleeding on the side of the road, waiting for death to extinguish his pathetic life.

He wasn't, he knew. He looked up and saw that something was not right with her, the massive dreaded woman. Bloody drool came forth from her lips and she looked at him stunned. She stood there, zombied by her own hand, her green eyes twice as wide as the second before. She had shot herself somehow.

He pushed her aside and ran out of the room.

And ran down the stairs and out of the house and into the street.

By the time he was pushing out the front door, he could hear her inaudibly screaming something, something that could have been anything, words, or nonlanguage, anguish squeezing itself through vocal cords and tearing into the world.

He tore down the street. He had forgotten his shoes and the concrete tugged at his naked soles with rawness.

■ ■ ■

He barely noticed how bloody his feet were when he stopped running. Even then he had no plan.

He decided at least to figure out where he was. He looked around him and saw people. A road sign. Princess Street. Probably Saturday, almost afternoon, judging from the crowd swarming downtown.

Someone had pointed a gun at him.

How long ago had that happened? An hour, two? Four?

Yesterday?

He had no shoes and no place to live.

He imagined he saw his father in the crowd and he ducked down a corner.

Even now he would not, could not go back.

The worst part was he knew by now his father would welcome him home, would just be happy to know that he was alright.

Was he alright?

He started walking towards the drug house, not knowing where else to go.

Halfway there, he turned around, thinking there may be others waiting to interrogate him. With guns. Perhaps friends of the dreadlocked girl, wanting revenge. Maybe the girl herself was there, bandaged up, waiting for him to show.

He went down an alleyway nearby and realized he was crying.

He was crying, but no water emerged from his eyes. His eyes were the desert. His eyes were so dry he knew that something must be wrong with them. He rubbed at them and rubbed at them.

But he only sobbed, moaned, whined, pitiful sounds escaped him, formed in his belly and bubbled up through his throat as if escaping an airlock, ripping their way out of him, on a tirade for survival.

He felt pressure on his shoulder. Someone was squeezing his shoulder. He looked up.

Smiley. Looking at him through his familiar mustache, frowning uncharacteristically. Ironically even.

"Hey," he sniffed out.

Smiley shook the shoulder he was laying pressure on. "Hey there."

Walter looked down at his hand. The pressure was uncomfortable, but he was grateful for it, grateful for the presence of someone other than himself, someone he actually knew.

Smiley cocked his head. "Where have you been?"

"Oh, just. I don't know. Around."

"Well, don't go back to my house." Smiley was somehow capable of calling it his "house" without sounding ironic, one of his many impressive abilities. "It's not safe there anymore. Something is happening."

"Something," Walter repeated stupidly. Some vague part of him recognized the terror spreading rapidly about him, but none of him was capable of truly grasping this was real.

Smiley nodded his head, as if Walter had contributed something extremely valuable to the one-sided conversation.

"Shit's going down," he said. "Big time. Has anyone asked you about me?"

Walter looked to the side, like he was intensely considering this. Then he shook his head. The sad thing was that he wasn't entirely lying; his brain simply wasn't working well enough to recount his recent experience.

"Good. Hopefully, we have a big enough head start on them."

"Head start?"

Smiley nodded again. "Come with me. We're leaving town."

"*Leaving*?"

Smiley began to pull Walter from the alleyway wall. Walter's body trailed ragdoll-like behind his grasp. "It's not safe here anymore. They're looking for me."

"Who?" Walter managed to cough up something, not repeated, an original thought blinking at the center of his melting brain. "Who is looking for you?"

Smiley was not giving Walter much attention anymore. Instead he was dragging him behind as he darted in a low, crouched position.

"Oh no one important," Smiley said. "Just drug dealers with guns."

CHAPTER X
On the Road

Walter had barely experienced travel before, maybe from the clear, safe, crisp passenger seat in the car for several hours, maybe in the plane sitting beside adult supervision while playing a handheld video game.

Now he bounced around the back of a strange man's van, holding on to the nothing to hold on to. Next to him Smiley slept, his head on one of the rungs of the van, his expression peaceful despite his cheeks vibrating along with the rockiness of the ride.

The van hit a bump and a pair of scissors flew up from somewhere. The bump caused Walter and Smiley both to spend a moment in the air. When they came down, Walter saw the scissors had sliced open Smiley's forearm.

His eyes remained closed.

Walter smacked him, yelling, "Your arm! Your arm! Stop the van!"

Smiley shrugged him off and opened his eyes.

"I know, I know, I felt it." His uninjured arm clutched the loose flap of skin where blood gushed through his fingers. "It's not a big deal. Cool your jets."

Walter looked at him, baffled, shook into quietness. "Are you serious? You're going to need stitches."

He shrugged and settled back down, shutting his eyes again, but his hand still loosely clutching the bloody arm.

"Your problem is you're too serious. Try and get some rest."

"But—"

"It's just blood," Smiley said, already halfway back into a bouncy dream. "It'll stop coming out, eventually."

CHAPTER XI
Arrival

"Get out of there! Bleeding all over my fucking van!"

The two young men were tossed from the dirty white vehicle one by one, landing in front of a dust-crusted gas station surrounded by tobacco fields, looking a couple steps up from an abandoned building.

The road sign was black marker on wood reading, *Gas and BBQ.*

Three splintery rocking chairs, one occupied by an elderly man, sat around the building, unrocking.

Smiley held his arm together with his reddened left hand, unperturbed as he lifted himself from the dirt and plopped alongside the old man in one of the chairs. A cloud of dust rose from the rotted wood, floating about his skeleton chest. The old man, also bare-chested, did not as much as shift in his seat at Smiley's presence beside him. The chiseled expression on his meltingly old face was unkillable.

Smiley looked at him, looked back at his arm, held it up for a better look, continuing to pinch the skin together in one hand. He set the wounded arm back down in his lap and relaxed and waited for Walter.

Walter still in the dirt. His cheeks muddy from dirt and his body's salty water. His right shoulder hurt badly from where he had hit the ground. He made no sound and then he did—a whine that lasted several seconds.

He picked himself up from the dust and joined Smiley in the other chair.

They sat there, the three of them for a while, without talking. The looks on their faces.

The dirty world operated around them, abandoned, wind

rustling up nothing but dust and pine straw in a demonstration of this hollowness, perhaps having died while the two of them had been distracted, traveling to this pointless destination, their arrival here as significant as someone's finger landing in one spot on a map of infinity.

Smiley sniffled, anything but dead, one of his nostrils sealed shut in fiery snot. He was grateful for the blood really—a cool, refreshing wiggly presence against his palm that assured him of life. Any wriggling form of life other than its absence. It was now cold.

An hour passed, or more. Walter picked a splinter from the rocking chair out of his finger. He scratched his hand with the same fingers that retained a shred or two of the woody blood. He felt himself calm down and settle into the landscape stretching around them.

The tobacco fields were as infinite as the sky.

Dusted shades of yellow, whir of winged insects. The emptiness of time passing.

The land smelled of dirt and worms and the hard, pointless work of men.

Somewhere along the line, Smiley's arm had stopped bleeding. The flab of raw skin glued to his arm looked grotesque but no longer gushed blood.

When Walter looked at him, he saw also that Smiley was unconscious in the chair, his head back and his jaw slung open, spittle bubbling up and beginning to make a gurgling sound.

Walter looked to the old man, taking him in. The many wrinkles in his shirtless chest made him look as though he had been infected with a disease that had caused him to sprout a thousand toothless mouths. There was a crossword puzzle in his lap and a pen on top.

He seemed oblivious to Walter and Smiley, rocking, his eyes barely as wide as slits in his face.

"Sir?" Walter said.

As he rocked, the pen rolled from his lap and to the earth. He made no move to pick it up.

"Sir?"

The old man's lips trembled, smacking each other, gearing up.

"I'm Walt. What's your name?"

"Roy," the old man said.

"Roy?"

"Roy."

"Roy, I think my friend could be hurt."

At the same instant he said this, Smiley's eyes snapped open. Wider than they had been, growing maybe in the arrival of consciousness, expanding.

"Where are we?"

Walter looked to his traveling companion, the twentysomething's hands brown with muddy blood.

"No idea," he said. "Some gas station somewhere."

"Gas station . . ." Smiley's face searched for something in his brain. "Beer."

Smiley stood from the chair and marched into the building.

He was not gone long enough for Walter to absorb the situation, the blank world around them. The world pulsed, it throbbed, the world was breathing slow and deliberate and raspy, as if dying.

Walter found a peace in it, in the tobacco fields staring back at him.

Smiley came back with a tremendous frown bending his face.

"That asshole won't sell me a drop. You have a license or something?"

"No," Walter said. He had let it expire a few years ago, and hadn't carried the old one on his person for at least a year.

"He says I need an ID. I'm practically thirty!" He rubbed some of the slimy hair above his lip.

Roy's head turned towards them. Walter expected it to crack and snap off with the movement. "How old is you, boy?"

Smiley looked to the old man, noticing him for the first time.

"You sure are ugly. Will you buy me beer?"

"They won't sell me no beer neither. 'Cause how I look."

Smiley's frown broke into his usual sarcastic grin. "You mean like you're gonna die or something?"

The old man's head turned to the crossword puzzle in his lap. His fingers twitched in his lap, fumbling with the paper. "How old is you, boy?"

"Pfff. I could be twenty-five. I don't really know and it doesn't fucking matter."

"You know, age don't mean much really. 'Live and dead's all there is."

"Yeah and you're pretty much the second one." Smiley grabbed Walter by the arm and started hauling him to his feet. Walter was surprised at how lifeless he had become in the past hour; his body was a floppy consciousness that sagged under Smiley's firm grip. A little bit of the dirty boy's blood dribbled onto Walter. Walter observed this happening, detached. He felt as if he had been set free at some silent moment in the past hour.

"You got a name?" the old man asked. His face seemed to be melting, twitching cheeks, moving but melting with the process, skin dripping down the crevices. The statue had come awake.

"Not really," Smiley said. He was dragging Walter behind them. Dust rose up around them. Smiley's thumb was already up with his arm, but they were not even to the road yet.

"No name and no age," said Roy behind them. His already quiet voice fading. "Sound pretty close to dead to me yourself."

■ ■ ■

They waited by the road, Walter having to concentrate to maintain his body from collapsing back into a pile of limbs, struggling to stand alongside Smiley, who stood, stiff as a post, his arm and thumb out.

When a trucker stopped not for them but for gas, Smiley harassed the overweight, bearded man to the point the man turned a deathly look on him, a look that said, I don't give a damn about you and your bloody arm.

After that they began to walk down the side of the road, both of their thumbs up now as Smiley had begun to insist.

The tobacco fields stretched on, watching but not caring in their dusty indifference. Everything had happened here and the two clownish young men were a tiny part of it, so small you couldn't see if you stared right at them.

The cars roared by in broken patterns of twos and threes, separated by the silence and the hum of insects in the fields.

There were maybe a handful of cars that Walter convinced himself were about to stop, but they did not.

A silver minivan seemed to be slowing behind them. Walter was sure the van was about to stop, but he became alarmed at the rising hope in him, knowing it was likely to be shot down again, dashed away, he and Smiley alone forever in the middle of the world, lost.

The minivan slid in front of them, close, stopping, screeching while transitioning from the pavement to the dirt, churning it up into mud.

"See!" Smiley said, the corner of his mouth twitching into a grin. "Here they are! Here is the person that will take us *home*."

Walter twitched at Smiley's ironic use of the term, home. Thinking of his father and of rooms where the air conditioner licked the sweat off his face.

A woman. Middle-aged and a forehead with stress tattooed into the creases, the eyes underneath watching them. Eyes that took notes.

"Boys," she said, cautious and in a voice that sort of attempted to assert itself.

She was a mother of a woman, overfull with the lie of her, the learned survival skills, all the necessary damage of raising more than one boy inflicted on her, the insecurities and the scars of her life visible and detectable. Though she might pathetically pretend.

To be someone else.

"I'm Jessica," she said. Her hair was a short blond, economic, cropped off in an attempt to air out the frustration of her life.

"Walter," he gasped out, still fighting to hold himself up along Smiley. One of his arms resting on Smiley's shoulder.

Smiley said nothing, but nodded at her.

"What happened to your arm?" She gaped.

"Nothing," Smiley said. He paused, the kind of pause that told you he realized what he had said was wrong and he was searching for the words to amend it. "Well. Scissors."

"Oh," she said. "Stitches?"

Smiley held up his arm and with his fingers lifted the loose flab of skin a quarter of an inch from the raw meat, stickily unattaching itself. He looked at her through the gap in between. And dropped the skin, letting the flab slap back into place.

"No thanks," he said. "I'm fine."

She grimaced. Her forehead crinkled, formulating a plan. "So you're Walter." She smiled at him, looking away from Smiley's deformity for a heartbeat. "And what is your name?" Returning her focus to the obviously more seasoned young hoodlum.

"Walter here calls me Smiley." He shrugged here. "You can too, if you want."

"Where are you two headed?"

"Wherever."

"Okay." She looked at him, a heap of concern that had already been there, purposeless and undirected, now finding meaning.

"Get in the van," she said.

■ ■ ■

Wheat hills tumbled and mingled into the next oncoming hill through the car window in Walter's limited field of view.

He was quiet.

Slowly, the fields turned into buildings. Small and rickety, and then bigger and more industrial.

"Where are we going?" came Smiley's voice from the seat behind him. He was up front, next to Jessica.

"Interesting that you are asking that question now," she said. Her posture was not averted from the road ahead.

Walter's head jerked slightly. He had begun to fall into sleep, drifting into that in between place where you forgot you were conscious.

The car coming to a stop. They were at a gas station—a real gas station this time with cars swarming about the pumps and rough-looking men loitering and smoking cigarettes by the door.

"Where are we going?" Smiley asked again, his enunciation identical to before, a replayed sound bite.

She did not look back to him, getting out of the car with a wallet in her hand. Her purse on the front seat, the wallet's usual home, near enough to Smiley that he could smell the leathery freedom.

"Well," she said, "*I*'m going home. Was on a work trip. The kids are waiting on dinner." She whipped a sparkling, plastic credit card from the wallet.

The car window down, the car off, her face no longer on him, she swiped her card, began to pump gas into her van. The gush of the gasoline swimming into her tank made a soft chugging sound, the vehicle greedily drinking its lifeblood.

"But I'm going to take you both somewhere *safe*," she said.

"No," Smiley replied calmly. He had clearly dealt with this sort of thing before.

Walter's ears perked up; he had not. He wasn't exactly sure what somewhere "safe" meant, but that didn't sound so bad.

"Look kid." Her voice drenched with self-importance, feigned or imagined power. "You don't get to just wander around, go where you want and do what you want. That's not how it works. Your arm all bloody like that. Jesus Christ."

"No," Smiley said again, with true authority.

"Oh yes." She still wasn't looking at him. He hadn't noticed before, or maybe she hadn't worn them before, but she had on sunglasses. The sun-bright world reflected on the lenses.

Smiley nudged Walter and gave him a wasted, devious expression that Walter could not read at all.

In Smiley's universe, there was nothing really left to do with this woman, other than to take what she had and leave her behind. That was what was next, that was all that was left. Smiley looked at her purse.

"Can I have a dollar?" he asked. "I want to get a drink at this gas station before you turn me over to the police."

Her expression grew concerned. "I'm not taking you to the police, Honey." An obvious lie from a very bad liar. She held out her hand, some green dollar bills revealing themselves between the leather mouth of her wallet. "Here you go. Get him something too. Whatever he wants." She nodded to Walter, who had become uninterested in the conversation and was again beginning to nod off.

A flicker of the hand. As he took the five, he pocketed a plastic debit card from her extended wallet in the same breath. Inside his pocket, Smiley rubbing the plastic between his fingers satisfactorily as he yanked Walter along beside him with the other hand.

"Wait," she said. "I'll go in with you."

But they were already gone, neither of them could barely hear her by then.

The gas station connected to a fast food restaurant with a maze of doors for restrooms, entering and exiting. There were enough people inside and around that the two of them were gone before she could have started looking.

He slipped in and out of the conjoined buildings and was walking down the road the other way.

Walter dragged along, starting to rise from his near comatose state.

He blinked.

He blinked again.

"Where is that lady, um, Jessica?" he asked, looking up at Smiley and his greasy mustache, ever moving, one hand firmly gripping Walter and essentially carrying him.

Smiley did not respond, continued to usher him along.

Walter shook his head, shook himself from Smiley's grip. At first he met resistance, and Smiley only held tighter, then when his shirt started to make the sound of tearing fabric and Walter did a little half whimper, half scream, Smiley released him.

Walter had stopped walking, Smiley's bare back to him continuing to plow on.

"What in the fuck is going *on*?" Walter demanded. "Stop walking away from me."

Walter looked around and saw that they were in a neighborhood, a neighborhood that had been gnawed on and chewed to shreds of graffitied concrete. He noted the crushed state of the housing surrounding them. Half of a paint smeared brick wall rose alongside them, the multicolored symbols and designs strewn across it abstract in meaning.

The projects.

A tall man in a grey hoodie and a pregnant woman wearing almost nothing stood nearby. The woman was talking too fast to be eavesdropped on.

"Smiley," Walter whispered, afraid of how loud he had been speaking before.

Smiley continued to plod forward.

Walter dashed to catch up with him, his heart hammering in his chest. They were in a dangerous neighborhood, a dangerous neighborhood that could be anywhere in North Carolina, as far as he knew.

Walter put a hand on Smiley's shoulder, trying to pull him back some, trying to study his eyes.

"Smiley, where are we?" he gasped.

Smiley was unperturbed, shaking off his hand and continuing to walk.

"Why did we not go with that lady? She seemed nice; I think she was going to help us."

Smiley finally stopped, turning to look Walter dead in the eye.

"You," he said, pausing, "are an idiot."

"Huh?"

"You don't have a clue! You do not have a clue about this world. Or what is going on in it. That woman was the enemy. We are at war Walt! We are at war, all the time in America. Suburbia and her kind is the enemy."

At the same time a gunshot sounded off somewhere and Walter felt the fear that he had suspected was building complete, born while he forgot to check for it, churning in his gut, eating his stomach.

Smiley turned back around, walking again, nonchalantly asking, "How was fucking that Kiwi girl?"

Walter cocked his head. "You never slept with her?"

"Well. Not exactly."

"I don't understand. She said she was your girlfriend."

"Sure. One of them. I don't exactly . . ."

"Are you gay?"

Smiley whirled back around, still walking though, backwards as he spoke to Walter. "Sure. That's really childish terminology. I have been fucked by men. But I'm not exactly normal."

Still walking backwards and facing Walter, he unzipped his ragged jean shorts and folded them out like the delicate opening of a book. Of course, he did not have on underwear.

"Oh."

Walter looked away immediately, closing his eyes and looking away and the image burned into his head, sizzling underneath where his brain was, the image a terrible part of him now, forever.

■ ■ ■

The sun slunk away. Night spread through the projects, deceptive in its slow gulping of the day.

Walter hurried his step, praying that Smiley did the same.

They did begin to enter a more commercial area.

A pawn shop.

A liquor store.

A gas station.

A row of hookers, disgusting in their ancient wrinkles, jeered at the two of them. Their clothes revoltingly exposed the age of their bodies, the toll of the lifestyle. All dressed in skirts and wearing clothes with bright neon colors of yellow, pink and orange, colors made to stand out against the night.

One of the ratty looking woman's breasts popped out of her top and stayed out, wrinkly and white even against the dark. She didn't try to tuck it back in, but wiggled her chest like her nipple was a deformed, miniature hand she waved at them.

"Over here boys . . ."

"You boys party?"

"Wanna a good time?"

"I'll suck your dick."

The voices were like the fluttering of crow wings, disorganized but together, joined and one mind in their hideous flavor.

The two of them walked.

Sirens. Blue lights flickered across his vision. Walter's heart thumped faster.

Behind them the hookers were being read their rights.

"Hey! Hey you two."

The police, the police were speaking to him. How had his life come to this?

He kept walking, speeding up. Trying to get ahead of Smiley. Maybe he could make them think he was not with Smiley, and Smiley would be the only one busted.

"HEY! You two stop right there!"

Walter stopped walking. Ahead of him Smiley had started running. A police officer was suddenly in front of Walter, a gun out, aimed at Smiley.

Walter felt metal biting into his wrists and was thrust to the ground.

"You shouldn't have run motherfucker." The voice boomed above Walter, flooding the night with authoritative prevalence.

Walter lifted his head up uncomfortably from the ground, watching. Another cop behind him was asking him questions he didn't hear.

The officer pulled the trigger.

Walter watched as Smiley's whole body shook and hit the ground.

The sound had not been like a gunshot, a sound Walter now knew.

Only a taser.

He was grateful for this realization, but after that he did not see Smiley. He felt himself being lifted from the ground.

He was shoved into the back of the police car with one of the prostitutes. She was ugly like all the rest of them, but there was something scarily familiar about her. He looked up at the shotgun mounted over both of their heads. And was afraid in a way previously unfathomable to him until that moment.

Without a word of explanation, the police car carried them on into the night.

Walter looked at the woman next to him. Why was she so familiar? How did he know her? Her wrinkled face wet with tears. Looking at her more closely, he saw she had been very pretty, maybe even just a couple years ago, before the drugs had started to set in. He saw track marks all up and down her arms, scab and leather. The shape of her was still feminine, she had not sacrificed womanhood for her lifestyle, only everything else.

Despite himself, despite his situation. Walter felt sorry for her. She was a woman who had fallen astray—nothing more and nothing less.

"What's the matter?" he asked her, meaning the tears.

"It's something about you. It reminds me of him," she said. "He would be about your age now. Or maybe a couple years younger. I haven't seen him in years."

"Who?"

"My son," she said. She let out a wail that cut the air like a physical thing. "Walter."

"Shut up back there," said the cop with his anger stamped so intently across his face, offering his glare of hate to them in the backseat for a moment. From where he sat, Walter watched the cop's fingernails digging into the rubber of the steering wheel with terror.

He looked back to his mother.

He felt he should scream at her, that he should somehow tangibly hand her everything that had happened in between then and the last moment he saw her, he felt that this had been a life, some form of one, that he had grown but ultimately not changed, led a life that was a product of hers in more ways than merely physiological. His voice made a fragile sound as in a dream where he attempted to scream and not a syllable came out.

He waited for the awfulness to pass. For the moment to disappear, to stand up and walk into that thing that didn't matter because it didn't really exist anywhere other than the erased parts of his mind—the past, *his* past.

He knew it would. Any second now.

EPILOGUE
The Boy Has Become the Man

The boy has become the man—

Though he cannot tell his psychiatrist when it happened—the brisk, business-like and somehow also casual man in ludicrously comfortable, squishy sweat pants, leaning back in his office chair and smiling the smile of the devil and looking younger than Walter in grey hair and not needing to nod or take notes—it *did* happen somewhere in time, in the time that Walter the man had been utterly raped by the years of his life. Ripped through them, along for the ride only.

Twenty-six—

But does it matter how old his body is? It has happened, the dream has passed into nightmare and he has not woken up still, beginning to suspect that he is operating in reality. He hasn't changed but he has. The part of him secret to him, the trickster, has made itself new without his knowledge. He discovered that life is the nightmare you do not emerge from even as you realize you are only wading through your own mind, finally giving up on wakefulness and surrendering to the horror, you wait to die but hoping you won't notice when you do.

But he has noticed it. Finally the child in him is dead and has been and will be.

"Walter?"

He is the change he has been noticing in the world, he finally realizes. Once believing himself separate from it, but now seeing this is not true. The world changes, folding in on itself and impounding gradually and expanding in the same breath, altering a detail each day.

"Are you paying attention?"

He changes with it. He looks down into his empty palms,

resting in his lap in front of where he waits for diagnosis on the couch stretching underneath him like landscape.

"Walter. You're not going to get anything out of this if you don't try. Answer the question."

His empty hands, expecting to find something there almost, something he holds that was forgotten.

The psychiatrist sighs in his office chair. The chair has wheels. He swivels toward Walter, his expression darkening.

He looks up and thinks back on every single thing. He has no idea what is about to happen.

The grey-haired man, receding hairline, optimistic attitude and all, stands up and slaps his patient in the face.

Walter looks up, blinking, certain this is a violation of something. Though it may or may not be the first time an employee of the psych ward has put hands on a client, it is almost certainly the first time Walter has heard of one with an MD doing it.

He touches his already sore cheek. His mouth warm with blood-tinged spit.

"What was the question, uh, sir?" Walter says, somehow managing to carry a tone of irony.

"What happened in the cop car? With your mother?"

"Nothing," he said.

"She didn't recognize you?"

"No."

"Not even later at the police station? You were brought in together. Did she recognize you then?"

"I didn't let her."

The psychiatrist rolls his eyes exasperatingly, then settles back down while scrawling something on a notepad in his lap that Walter is only noticing now. Certainly he has written on this sheet of paper that Walter is beyond human aid.

"That's not possible, of course," the psychiatrist adds nonchalantly.

Walter looks up curiously. "Why is that?" he asks.

"Because it was her who admitted you. You've been living with her since then."

Walter takes a moment to think about this, more intrigued than disturbed.

"Alright, alright. That is enough for this session." The psychiatrist wheels his chair away.

Despite himself, Walter smiles. He has absolutely no idea what is about to happen and the idea of this comforts him. Probably for the first time.

　　　■　■　■

The things that have happened to him. Really only existing in between his ears, skewed and slightly different as he reconjured them, vomiting each piece over the past few days for the evaluation, beginning with the memory of Katherine, with beauty and water, his mother drinking over his bedside, his father and the beach and the cigarettes secretly smoked on the porch, all the way up to his adventures with the hermaphroditic homeless twentysomething.

How could these be the things that make him? These fragile things, barely able to maintain a consistent shape.

So what has happened to his life?

Where has it gone while he wasn't looking?

He blinked and missed it, closing his eyes a boy—a blink that lasted thirteen years. He opens them now.

An adult body, the soul of a man in it. Sleeping in a room, rubber sheets. Waiting for his life to run dry.

Waiting.

He waits to die, unconvinced he will.

www.ingramcontent.com/pod-product-compliance
Lightning Source LLC
Chambersburg PA
CBHW050403110726
47899CB00008B/2633